THE #1
SPORTS SERIES
FOR KIDS

®

BODY CHECK

LITTLE, BROWN AND COMPANY
Books for Young Readers
New York   Boston

Little, Brown and Company

Hachette Book Group USA
237 Park Avenue, New York, NY 10017
Visit our Web site at www.lb-kids.com

www.mattchristopher.com

First Edition: November 2003

Library of Congress Cataloging-in-Publication Data

Hirschfeld, Robert.
    Body check : the #1 sports series for kids / Matt Christopher ;
text by Robert Hirschfeld — 1st ed.
       p. cm.
    Summary: Twelve-year-old Brent Mullen discovers that the new
assistant hockey coach is teaching the defensemen on his team
illegal moves to help them win at any cost
       ISBN 978-0-316-13405-7
   [1. Sportsmanship —Fiction. 2. Hockey — Fiction.
   3. Cheating — Fiction. 4. Winning and losing — Fiction.]
I. Christopher, Matt   II. Title.
PZ7.H59794Bo 2003
[Fic] — dc21   2002043338

PB: 10 9 8 7 6 5

COM-MO

Printed in the United States of America

1

Brent Mullen looked closely at the blade of his left skate. He felt the edges with his thumb to see if it needed sharpening. He decided to ask his father or older brother to take him to the skate store that afternoon, or tomorrow at the latest.

Brent was twelve and played right wing for his hockey team, the Badgers. Brent was tall and rangy and kept his brown hair trimmed short. He wished that he could put on some more weight — more muscle, anyway — but figured, if he did, he wouldn't be as fast and shifty on the ice. Brent knew that his greatest asset as a hockey player was his skill at making quick turns and stops.

That was why he made sure to get his blades sharpened weekly, at least. Like all skate blades, his had a slight hollow between the edges. Brent liked that

1

hollow to be a little deeper than most because he thought it helped him maneuver better. He'd read that his idol, Mario Lemieux, did the same thing.

As he began lacing up, someone poked him in the shoulder. A familiar, husky voice said, "Yo, dude, what's happening?"

His friend Cam Johanssen plopped himself down on the rinkside bench next to Brent. Cam was stocky, with powerful legs, and wore his light blond hair in a buzz cut. Cam was a defenseman. Unlike Brent, who preferred to stay out of the way, Cam enjoyed hitting. He wasn't as good a skater as Brent, never scored, and rarely took a shot. But he was great at bodychecking.

"Hey, it's a contact sport," he'd say.

And since Brent didn't like hitting or being hit by others, he was glad to have a guy like Cam on his team to back him up. Also, he knew that even though Cam could and did slam into opponents, he never played dirty.

"You missed stretches today," Brent said as he worked on his laces. Every Badger practice began and ended with stretching.

"Yeah, our car wouldn't start," Cam said, putting on

his skates. "I saw Coach in the dressing room. He really chewed me out."

Brent stared at his friend. "No kidding?"

Cam snickered. "*Sure,* I'm kidding! Can you see Coach yelling at anyone? Ever?"

Coach Maxwell, who'd been in charge of the Badgers for years, was an easygoing man. Brent had never seen him lose his temper. His seventeen-year-old brother, Lee, had been a Badger years before, and he had never seen the coach yell at anyone for any reason. But that was okay with Brent. He liked Coach Maxwell.

Cam shook his head. "Maybe if the coach got mad once in a while we'd be a better team, you know?"

Brent laughed. "That doesn't make sense. How would we be better?"

Cam yanked at his laces to make sure they were tight. "Sure it makes sense! A team is sort of like its coach. When the coach gets mad sometimes, the team will, too. Maybe we'd play harder, be tougher. Instead, we're like Coach Maxwell. We're . . . you know . . . *nice.* Nobody's afraid of us. The coach doesn't push us. So, we lose as many as we win. We did last year, and we will this year, too."

3

Brent started to argue, but then he stopped. Cam was probably right. So far this season, the Badgers were 1 and 1. They'd probably split the rest of the games as well.

"You know what?" Brent said. "That's okay with me. I like Coach Maxwell. Maybe he isn't the kind of guy who yells and pushes all the time, but he knows the game. He's a good teacher. My brother, Lee, says that Coach Maxwell made him a good hockey player, and now Lee's one of the best high-school players in the county. If he can do the same thing for me, I don't care if we aren't league champs."

Cam shrugged. "Well, I like to win. I mean, why else keep score, you know? And where is the coach, anyway? Isn't it time for practice to start?"

"I think he's coming now," Brent said as the door from the locker room to the rink opened. Sure enough, Coach Maxwell came through the door, but he wasn't alone. There were two strangers with him, another man and a boy about their age, who was wearing skates and pads.

"You know those two?" he asked Cam.

"Unh-unh." Cam shook his head. The other Badgers, who had been chatting and getting ready to start practice, stopped talking and watched as the coach and the newcomers came toward them. Coach Maxwell raised his fingers to his lips and whistled.

"Everyone, group up over here," he called. The Badgers gathered around their coach, staring at the new boy, who stared back, not smiling. Brent figured he had to be nervous.

"Guys, meet Mr. Seabrook and his son, Vic," said the coach. The father waved and grinned. Vic nodded but still didn't smile. "They're new in town. Mr. Seabrook played a lot of hockey in his day, and he coached youth hockey where they used to live. Vic, here, played for his dad.

"As you know, I've been looking for someone to work with me coaching the Badgers, so having Mr. Seabrook show up is a stroke of good luck, I think. He's been nice enough to volunteer to work as my assistant. And Vic will join the Badgers as a player."

Coach Maxwell studied Vic for a moment. "You look to me like a defenseman, am I right?"

Vic muttered, "Yeah, that's right."

"Well, good, fine," said the coach. "That's settled, then. Vic, you have all your pads and a stick?"

The boy nodded again.

Cam poked Brent. "He sure talks a lot."

Brent started to laugh but managed to turn it into a cough.

"Great," said the coach. "You can work out with us today."

"If it's all right with you, Coach Maxwell," said Mr. Seabrook, "I'd like to watch today. Just get a look at the team."

"Very good," said the coach. "We'll talk later on." He turned to the players. "Okay, let's get going. Vic, if you have any questions, ask me or one of the other guys. But I think you'll find most of what we do is a lot like what you were used to with your old team. We'll start with our usual skatearound, then some end-to-ends."

The Badger players skated onto the rink and began circling it. Cam came up alongside Brent. "Maybe this new coach will fire our team up a little more." He spoke just loud enough so that only Brent could hear him.

Brent kept his own voice down, too. "Maybe. And it won't hurt to have another defenseman, either. You guys could use a little more backup."

"Oh, yeah?" Cam said. "Seems to me that our defense is fine . . . if only we could score a couple more goals now and then." Brent looked at Cam and both boys grinned to show that they were only joking.

After the team had taken several laps around the rink to warm up, Coach Maxwell set two orange traffic cones near one end of the rink, about fifteen feet apart. "Split into two groups and form two lines down at that end of the ice," he called.

When the team had divided into equal groups he said, "Okay, this is a speed drill in the form of a relay race. Vic, since you're new today, I'll explain: the first guy in each group skates full-speed to this end of the ice, around this cone, and back to the starting point. When he touches the board at that end, the next guy in line takes off. Questions? Okay. This is about *speed* and *control.* First two ready? Set? And . . . *go!*"

Brent, one of the fastest skaters, was the anchor skater of his group. He yelled encouragement to the skaters before him, including Cam. Cam pumped hard but wasn't fast, and he lost ground to his opponent when he slowed down to make the turn around the cone. So Brent's side was a few yards behind when the next two, including Vic on the other side, took off.

Watching Vic, Brent winced. The new guy was

seriously *slow*. Maybe his skates needed sharpening, because he slipped and almost stumbled at the turn. By the time he finished, he had not only lost the lead but was trailing by a few feet.

When Brent got going, the two sides were even. Brent got into a forward lean, swinging his arms freely, noting in the corner of his eye that his opponent was right with him. As he neared the cone, Brent decided to use a fast, slightly risky crossover turn. Moving to the right of the cone, he leaned his body left with his inside, left leg bent at the knee. He pushed off hard with his right leg and quickly swung it across his left leg, pivoting his body so that he was ready to head the other way. It gave him a three-foot lead on the player in the other lane, and he was able to hold that lead as he streaked to the finish.

"Way to go," Cam shouted, wrapping Brent in a bear hug. "You can motor, dude!"

Shortly afterward, the coach and a couple of players moved some cones into a "slalom" course for players to work on turns. For Brent, this was easy. Cam had trouble.

"Cam, shorten your stride a little and you get better control," called the coach. Cam did as he'd been told. "See? Much better!"

Vic had a lot of trouble making the turns at all. "Hang in there, big fella!" his father called out, clapping his hands.

As Vic finished the course, looking embarrassed, Coach Maxwell came up, put his arm around the boy's shoulders, and spoke quietly to him. Vic nodded several times.

Brent leaned toward Cam. "Bet he's telling Vic that his blades are too dull."

Cam snorted. "That's the least of his problems. But you're right. You'd think he would have known to do that."

The coach whistled for attention. "Right, let's go through the slalom again — backwards this time."

Hockey players must skate backward as well as forward, and defensemen like Cam were more comfortable with this drill. Even Vic got through the backward exercise without serious problems, though he was still slow.

A little later, Coach Maxwell said they'd work on passing. He looked at Mr. Seabrook. "Any passing drills you like?"

The other man held up his hands. "Today I'm just an observer."

The coach had pairs of players skate up and down the rink, passing the puck back and forth. He had them work on backhand passes and drop passes, where a player "drops" the puck for a player coming from behind or alongside. The coach stopped the action now and then to give suggestions. Mr. Seabrook stood just off the rink, clapping his hands a lot and shouting out things like "All right," "Way to go!" or "That's the old hustle!" Brent wasn't very impressed by him and said so to Cam during a break in practice. Cam waved it off.

"The guy is new. Cut him a little slack."

After the break, the coach organized a passing-and-defense game called Monkey in the Middle. Three players went to each of the five face-off circles painted on the ice. The circles were ten yards across, with face-off spots in the middle. Two passers stood outside each circle and the third — the defender — stood at the face-off spot. The passers hit the puck to each other, going around the circle, and the defender tried to intercept. When a defender got the puck, he became a passer, and the player whose pass was picked off went into the middle. Coach Maxwell roamed among the groups, watching each in turn.

Brent's group included a center named Ted and Vic as defender. Brent and Ted passed the puck between themselves for a while, and Vic seemed unable to do anything to stop them. Brent began to feel weird, as if he and Ted were being unfair. Vic looked helpless.

Then, just after Ted had gathered in a pass from Brent, Vic lunged forward in his direction. Ted looked startled as Vic charged at him, and he froze for a second. Brent couldn't see exactly what happened next, since Vic's body blocked his view. But the next thing he knew, Ted had fallen to the ice, and Vic had the puck on his stick and was grinning triumphantly.

Coach Maxwell, who had been watching another group, hurriedly skated over to see if Ted was hurt. Brent stared at Vic, who paid no attention to the fallen player.

Instead, Vic and his father looked at each other for a second.

Quickly — so quickly that Brent wasn't sure what he had seen — the man nodded to his son. And the son's grin got even wider.

2

Ted slowly got to his feet. He shook his head, as if he had been a little stunned, and looked at Coach Maxwell. "I'm okay," he said.

"Go to the bench and sit a minute," said the coach. "Let's make sure you're all right."

As Ted slowly skated to the side of the rink, Brent asked him, "You sure you're okay?"

Ted nodded. "I just slipped, that's all."

"How'd it happen?" Brent asked. "It looked to me like Vic ran into you."

"Maybe we got tangled up a little bit," said Ted as he left the ice. He looked to make sure that Vic wasn't too close by. "I mean, the guy isn't the most coordinated athlete, is he?"

"So it was an accident?" Brent asked. Vic still hadn't come to see if Ted was okay.

Ted sat on the bench and rubbed his arm. "Huh? Sure it was an accident. I mean, what else could it have been?"

Brent, who had seen the look that passed between Vic and Mr. Seabrook, wasn't so sure. But he didn't say anything else.

Once it was clear that Ted hadn't been injured, practice continued. Later on, the coach set up a three-on-two drill, where a center and two wings tried to get a shot on goal against two defenders. Brent, playing right wing on one squad, thought he might be able to get in behind Cam, who was defending. But Cam saw Brent try to move in on the goal and made a quick recovery, getting his stick on the center's pass and poking it away.

"Good move," Brent admitted. "Thought I had you there."

"Good anticipation, Cam," called Coach Maxwell. "Nice poke check!"

Mr. Seabrook clapped his hands. "Way to hustle, fella!"

A little later, Vic was in another group, as a defender. Barry, a speedy wing, got past Vic and looked like he might have a breakaway goal opportunity. Vic lunged for him, and Coach Maxwell stopped the action with a whistle.

"That's what we call hooking, Vic," he said calmly. "In a game, you'd have gone to the penalty box for two minutes, and the other team would have a power-play opportunity."

"Aw, come on!" Vic said. He was going to say more, but his father broke in, sharply.

"*Vic!* Never argue with your coach."

Vic looked at the ice and muttered, "Yeah." He didn't look happy.

"We'll talk about this later," said Mr. Seabrook, glaring at his son. He looked at Coach Maxwell. "Sorry, Coach."

The coach nodded. "Play on," he said.

Brent went over to Cam, watching from the sideline. "What did you think of that?"

"Think of what?" asked Cam.

"What just happened." Brent leaned in closer and kept his voice to a whisper.

Cam shook his head. "Huh? Vic was out of position, and when he tried to recover, his stick caught Barry's leg. You never saw anyone called for hooking before?"

"I don't know. First he knocks Ted down, and then

14

he hooks Barry. And did you hear Mr. Seabrook? He wasn't angry at the hooking, just that Vic talked back to the coach!"

Cam stared at Brent. "The guy's a bad skater. He probably ran into Ted by accident. Then, he didn't play his position right and made it worse by doing something stupid. He's a bad hockey player, is all. I bet Vic won't get much ice time in games."

Brent said, "I think what happened to Ted *wasn't* an accident. Also, I think Mr. Seabrook saw it and liked what he saw."

Cam let a second go by. Then he said, "That's pretty heavy. You tell anyone else?"

"Unh-unh," answered Brent, "just you."

"Good. If you're smart, you *won't* say anything to anyone else. I think you're totally out of line."

Brent asked, "Really?"

"Yeah," Cam replied. "You're saying Vic's a goon and Mr. Seabrook is worse, and you don't have much to go on. Do you?"

"Well . . . maybe not."

Cam nodded. "We know Vic's clumsy, that he's a bad skater. He bumped Ted by accident. Hooking Barry was just bad hockey."

"I guess," Brent admitted.

"And nothing Mr. Seabrook said or did *proves* he's a creep. Right?"

Brent sighed. "Okay, you're right. I'm not being fair."

Cam smiled at his friend. "If it was me coming into a new place, I'd hope nobody did to me what you're doing to these two. Give them a chance."

"All right," Brent agreed. "I will."

Coach Maxwell often used the end of practice to work on power plays and penalty killing. When a player is called for a foul and sent to the penalty box, usually for two minutes, the opponents have a one-player advantage. In that case, they'll go to a power play. The team with the penalized player will try to "kill" the penalty and not give up a goal while they're down a player.

"We'll use the umbrella formation for a power play today," the coach said. He put Ted in the middle of the rink, just in front of the blue line that separates the team's offensive zone from center ice. Brent and Sandy, another wing, went to either side of Ted, and two other forwards set up near the goal, one on each side.

"The idea is to make quick passes between the pivot and the wings," said the coach. "You may force the defense into an error and create an opening for an out-side shot. Or maybe one of the guys near the goal might be left open. If so, get him the puck.

"The problem is, there's no one back on defense except the goalie. If a defender intercepts a pass, he might go all the way and maybe score a shorthanded goal. Be careful with your passes. Now, let's put a defense out there."

He placed four defenders, including Cam and Vic, in a diamond formation, with Cam by the pivot man, one defender on each side, and one player in front of the goalie.

The coach said, "Think of zone defense in basket-ball. Each defender guards an area. Don't overload one side, or the offense can pass to where the defense is thin and get a shot. If you get the puck, just shoot it down toward their goal. Make them use penalty time skating back to recover it. The idea of penalty killing is to deny them shots on goal for two minutes. I'll give Ted the puck and call time after two minutes — unless there's a goal. Ready . . . *go!*"

Ted slapped a pass to Brent. Brent saw that the for-wards near the goal weren't open, so he passed back to Ted, skating down the ice as he did. Ted fired a backhander to Sandy, who tried to get the puck to Brent. But Cam darted forward, took the puck, and rocketed it down to the other goal, forcing Ted to retrieve it.

"Good D!" called Coach Maxwell.

"Way to go!" added Mr. Seabrook.

On their next try, Cam made a mistake and skated directly in front of Chip, the goalie, blocking his view of the play. Brent flipped the puck to Ted, who sent a lightning-fast puck to the wing just left of the goalmouth. He slipped the puck past the goalie's stick for a goal.

Coach Maxwell whistled, and play stopped. "You have to stay in the zone you're guarding, or problems happen. Cam, you see what went wrong there?"

Cam nodded, grinning sheepishly. "I went too far across and got in Chip's way."

"Okay, that's how we learn," the coach said. "Let's get another group on the ice."

"Coach, if you like, I'll take these guys to the other end while you work with the rest," offered Mr. Seabrook.

"Okay," said Coach Maxwell.

Mr. Seabrook went to the end of the rink with the first group. He gave Ted the puck to start play. Ted and the two wings passed the puck around, looking for an opening, but the defenders stayed put, and no shots were possible for the first thirty seconds.

Ted sent the puck to Sandy, a good stick-handler. Sandy moved in on Vic, hoping to bring Vic toward him so he could pass to a player near the goal or take a shot himself. But Vic suddenly charged Sandy, who was caught by surprise. Before Sandy could pass or shoot, Vic rammed him with a shoulder and raised forearm. Staggering, Sandy avoided falling but lost control of the puck.

Brent waited for Mr. Seabrook to say or do something about the obvious foul. Mr. Seabrook clapped and said, "Way to hustle, guys! Let's set up again."

It looked to Brent as if Sandy might speak up, but he didn't. Nobody else said a word. Had Brent been the only one to see it?

He decided he'd better say nothing. Without someone to back him up, he didn't want to make trouble. But this time, he was sure. Vic committed a foul, and Mr. Seabrook — *Coach* Seabrook — did nothing.

A little while later, Coach Maxwell called, "Okay, that's it. Let's stretch." While the players stretched, the coaches talked quietly.

Afterward, Coach Maxwell said, "Starting tomorrow, Coach Seabrook will spend part of every practice working with the defense and goalies while I stay with the forwards. He was a defense specialist in his playing days. Coach, care to say anything?"

Mr. Seabrook smiled brightly. "I'll only say that I look forward to working with you boys and helping you be winners."

Winners. Somehow, this didn't sound right to Brent. Coach Maxwell never emphasized winning. He stressed teamwork and doing your best. Winning was nice, when it happened, but was that really the bottom line?

As he changed into his street clothes, he didn't take part in the usual locker-room chatter. He was still quiet when he and Cam went to wait for Cam's mother to pick them up.

Cam finally said, "What's going on? You haven't said a word since we left the ice."

"Nothing's wrong," Brent said.

"Uh-huh," Cam replied. "Something's on your mind, I know it. Come on, spit it out."

Brent shook his head. "Well, okay, but you won't like it. It's the Seabrooks."

Cam rolled his eyes. "Here we go again."

Brent described what Vic had done to Sandy. "His father was right there and saw it, and he didn't do anything."

"Shoulder checks are legal," Cam pointed out. "I use them all the time."

"Not when you use a raised forearm, too. That's a foul," Brent said. "That's what Vic did. Didn't you see it?"

"Hey, I was busy guarding people," Cam said. "What about Sandy? He didn't complain. Nobody else did, either."

"I know," said Brent. "But I saw what I saw. This time, I'm right."

Cam scratched his head. "Okay, I know you're not crazy. Maybe Vic did what you say he did, and maybe his father didn't call him on it. Maybe Mr. Seabrook didn't want to make trouble for his son, or something, I don't know. But all I can say is, I think you should just be cool and see how things go. That's what I'm

21

going to do. Maybe everything will turn out to be all right. If it doesn't, then . . . well, I don't know. But for now, why not wait and see?"

Brent nodded. "Guess you're right. That's the best way to go."

One thing was for sure. He *hoped* he was wrong about the Seabrooks.

3

When Brent had a problem, he usually discussed it with his big brother, Lee, especially if the problem concerned hockey. Lee was the star center on his high-school team. He was their leading scorer and was almost sure to be the team captain when he became a senior next year.

So that evening after dinner, Brent asked Lee if he could talk to him.

"Sure," Lee answered. "Come on upstairs." They went to Lee's room, which had posters on the walls of Lee's favorite players, Wayne Gretzky, Bobby Orr, and Mark Messier.

"I figured something was on your mind at dinner when you only had two helpings of chicken," Lee said. "What's up?"

"It's about this new guy on the team," said Brent.

"Well, him and his father. Cam says I'm making a big deal out of nothing, but I don't think so. Only, maybe he's right, I don't know. Maybe I'm unfair. Except I haven't really made a big deal, not yet, anyway —"

Lee held up a hand. "Whoa, slow down! Start from the beginning and take your time."

Brent explained about the arrival of Mr. Seabrook and his son, and what Vic had done, or *might* have done, that day at practice. He also talked about the way Mr. Seabrook had ignored Vic's obvious fouls.

"And now he'll be coaching with Coach Maxwell. When he talked to us, he said he'd help us become 'winners.' Coach Maxwell says that if you give it your best and play as a team, you're a winner no matter what the score is."

"Maybe that's what Mr. Seabrook meant," Lee suggested. "Is that possible?"

This hadn't occurred to Brent. "Maybe," he said. "But I don't think so. Cam probably thinks that's the way it is."

"Cam's right about one thing, for sure," said Lee. "You don't want to go off half-cocked about this. Coach Maxwell would probably say the same thing."

Brent nodded. "Yeah, I know. It's just . . . I get a feeling about them."

Sitting on his bed, Lee leaned back against the wall. "Well, I know that there are people in hockey who don't believe in playing by the rules, if they can get away with it. Players, coaches, parents, fans — they're out there. I haven't come across a lot of them. A few are bad enough, of course. Still, I don't think there are a lot of rotten apples."

"Did you ever meet guys like that — you know, goons — with the Badgers?"

Lee shook his head. "Nope. I heard about teams that were supposed to play dirty, but they were never in our league."

"How about now? In school?"

Lee thought about it. "There are guys we call enforcers. They're usually not real good in basic skills. They aren't fast or good stick-handlers; they don't shoot well or get many assists. You know. So they try to make up for what they can't do by hitting hard. They'll slam into the other team, hip checks, shoulder checks, whatever.

"But even enforcers usually play clean. They may be

rough, but they play by the rules. We have guys like that, and you know what? I'm glad. Some teams try to intimidate you early in games by laying some big hits on you. When you have an enforcer, you can send them a message: *It won't work. You'll have to outplay us, because you can't out-tough us.* Hey, hockey's a physical sport. You get going really fast, people bang into each other, sometimes people lose their cool a little. That's the game, and enforcers have a place in it. But dirty players and cheaters don't."

Brent said, "I can understand that."

Lee added, "Maybe this new coach just wants your team to stand up against more aggressive teams. Could that be what he's saying when he talks about being winners?"

"I guess," answered Brent, not at all sure. "It sounds like you're saying I should wait and see, for now."

"Don't you think that's the best thing to do?" asked Lee.

Brent said, "But what if I'm right about Vic and Mr. — *Coach* Seabrook. What then?"

Lee chewed his lower lip. "Well, if it turns out you're right, more people will see for themselves. Coach Maxwell really knows the game. He's still the smartest hockey coach I ever met. He'll know if something isn't the way it ought to be, and so will other players. Probably some parents, too. You'll find that you won't be alone in wanting something to be done to fix the problem. *If* there's a problem."

Brent suddenly felt better. "Yeah. I guess what was bothering me was I thought it was all on me, that I was alone. But if stuff keeps happening, then I won't be alone, will I? That's good to remember."

"No, you'll have people standing up with you, I guarantee it," Lee said. "And don't forget, it may turn out that you were wrong and that they're really okay. There's a good chance of that."

"I hope so," said Brent. "Yeah, Vic may just turn out to be our enforcer. I mean, he sure isn't much of a skater."

"It's like I said," his brother pointed out. "Enforcers usually aren't fantastic skaters. Maybe his dad figures that Vic will do better if he plays physical, aggressive hockey. That could be his whole deal, you know? He's just trying to look out for his son."

Brent smiled. "I understand that, if that's what he wants. According to Coach Maxwell, Mr. Seabrook was a defenseman when he played. I guess it wouldn't hurt to have a defensive-minded coach to work with Coach Maxwell."

"Absolutely not," agreed Lee.

Brent stood up. "Thanks," he said. "I feel a lot better. I'll tell Cam what you said. And I hope that it turns out that Vic is a nice guy who just needed a little time to get used to being here."

"I hope so, too," said Lee.

4

Cam was buckling his shin pads when Brent sat down next to him in the locker room. The two friends usually suited up together.

"Hey!" Cam said, reaching for his other pad. "What's up?"

"Nothing much." Brent began pulling gear out of his athletic bag. "Oh, yeah, I wanted to tell you, I talked to Lee last night. About . . . you know . . ."

"Yeah, I know," said Cam. "And?"

Just then, Vic walked by with his bag on one shoulder and his stick over the other. The two watched him go. Brent told himself to keep an open mind about Vic, but there was something that rubbed him the wrong way, even in Vic's walk . . . a kind of swagger.

Brent said, "Lee agrees that I'm making too much out of too little."

29

Cam grinned. "I always knew Lee was a smart guy. So, now are you convinced?"

"Yeah." Brent sat down, keeping his voice low. "Well, actually, you pretty much convinced me yesterday. But I just wanted to talk to Lee anyway. I mean, he knows the game better than I do."

"So you're not going to go around bad-mouthing Vic and his dad? You'll give them a chance?" Cam asked.

"Right, that's what I said." Brent felt a little annoyed at Cam. After all, he hadn't "gone around bad-mouthing Vic and his dad," all he'd done was talk quietly to Cam and Lee. It wasn't like he'd tried to get Vic thrown off the team. But he hoped his irritation didn't show as he said, "I want to ask you one thing."

"Yeah? What?"

"If you notice anything that makes it look like I was right . . . tell me, okay?"

Cam frowned. "You still don't sound like you're convinced."

"I said I'd keep my mind open," Brent replied. "I'm asking you to do the same thing."

"Sure," Cam said. "Hey, I don't want anyone on the team who doesn't follow rules, any more than you do.

For one thing, it'll hurt the team. For another, I don't like it."

"Okay, then," Brent said. They finished putting on their protective gear and workout clothes but left their skates off until the team had gone through their stretching routine.

Coach Maxwell led the stretching himself. He liked to say that it was the best insurance against injury. The players gathered in a cleared-out section of the locker room, where they could lie full-length on the floor. They went through a dozen exercises designed to keep their ligaments and muscles flexible. Coach Seabrook, wearing sweats and carrying a whistle, watched and once in a while said things that were meant to sound encouraging. "That's it, work it out," and "Way to go!"

Brent thought he sounded silly, but he decided that the guy wanted to be helpful. At one point, after Coach Seabrook said, "Yeah! Work those hammies," he and Cam caught each other's eyes and just barely managed to avoid giggling.

"Okay, lace up your skates and get on the ice," called Coach Maxwell. The workout began as it always did, with a skatearound to warm up. The players would

31

take laps around the rink, first going forward and then backward. Brent smiled, remembering how tough skating backward had been for him when he first went out for hockey at the age of seven. Lee, who was with the Badgers at the time, had been very patient and helped him a lot.

"It's going to feel funny at first," his big brother had said, "but you'll get used to it."

"Why do I have to go backward?" Brent remembered asking. "I'm going to be a center like you, not play defense."

"Every hockey player has to do it," Lee had explained. "Even wings and centers play defense when the other team has the puck. And defense means skating backward. Come on, it's no big deal. Bend your knees, like you're going to sit in a chair . . . good! Now, use the inside edge of your right skate to push yourself backward . . . then straighten out your right leg, and . . . *oops!* Okay, you're not hurt, get up and try again. All right, good! Now shift your weight to your left leg and use *that* skate to push yourself back, and . . . *uh oh!* Okay, up you go and try it again . . ."

Brent's rear end had been sore for a while before he mastered the trick, but Lee was right, of course: once

Brent got the idea, it became automatic. Not that Brent could skate backward as fast as Cam or most defensemen, who usually skate backward more than wings and centers. Brent sometimes teased Cam that Cam could go faster backward than forward.

After the skatearound, Coach Maxwell split the team into pairs for a passing drill, focusing on lead and drop passes. One player of each pair starts from the end of the rink, and his partner gives him a twenty-foot lead before following him, taking the puck. The puck-handler skates to the first blue line and fires a fore-hand pass to his teammate, who receives the pass and skates toward the red line that divides the ice in half before leaving a drop pass for the first man. The first player then fires the puck at the unguarded goal. The two come back the other way, reversing roles as they do so.

Coach Maxwell watched from rinkside and made suggestions to players: "Use more follow-through on your forehand pass, Sandy," or "Vic, try not to shoot when your weight is on the foot closer to the puck, or you'll have trouble controlling your shot. Shoot when you're planted on the other foot."

Afterward, the coach set up a drill to work on flip

shots, where a shooter lofts the puck into the goal over an obstacle, like a goalie's stick, arm, or leg. For this drill, Coach Maxwell put a six-inch-wide board across the goalmouth for the team to shoot over.

"Remember," he said, "you have to bring the tip of your blade — what we call the *toe* — close to the puck and use both wrists to flick the puck, like *this*." The coach demonstrated, flipping the puck over the board and into the cage. "All right, give it a try."

One by one, the Badgers tried their own flip shots. Brent did pretty well, he thought, but Coach Maxwell said, "Don't use the stick like a shovel, Brent. That was more of a scoop than a flip. See what I mean?"

Brent nodded and tried again. "Much better," said the coach. "You have strong wrists, so take advantage of them."

Next, the two coaches had a slap-shot practice. At either end of the rink a coach set up a line of pucks about three feet apart. A player skates along the line, winds up, and smashes each puck in turn at the un-guarded goal.

"More windup," Coach Maxwell told one Badger. "Don't just push the puck, Ted. There's a reason it's called a slap shot. . . . That's it! It's not a shot you'll use too often, because it's not accurate," he told the team, "but when you do use it, you want to really whack that puck. Remember, slap shots are for situations when there's an opening that is likely to close up fast; otherwise, use a standard forehand or backhand shot."

After the shooting drill, the coach had players take a break. "Afterward, we'll split up. Defensemen and goalies will work with Coach Seabrook, and the rest of you, stay with me."

"Goalies, put on all your gear," Coach Seabrook called out. "Masks, blockers, everything. Okay?"

A hockey puck is a disk made of hard rubber. If it hits a player, it can really hurt, especially if it strikes an unprotected part of the player's body. Nobody has more pucks flying at them than goalies. That's why, in games, a goalie wears a mask to protect his face. But the mask is designed for safety and not for comfort. A goalie also wears much more other gear than the rest of a hockey team: bulky thigh and knee pads and pants with extra padding. On the hand that holds the stick handle, he wears a rectangular pad called a blocker, a device with which he can block shots without getting bruised forearms. On his other hand, he wears a catching glove, like a heavy version of a first baseman's mitt in baseball. This, too, he uses to block or even catch pucks.

A goalie must wear this gear to keep from being injured in games and whenever shots will be coming at him, but Coach Maxwell usually let the goalies practice without heavy gear, when pucks wouldn't be flying at them.

Brent was surprised when Coach Seabrook told the goalies to put on their full gear. The team wasn't going to scrimmage right now. Brent saw that Chip, the Badgers first-string goalie, a guy who usually wore a smile that wouldn't quit, wasn't happy about having to put on what he called "his suit of armor" just to work out with the defense. But he didn't say anything. When a coach says "jump," you don't whine about it, you just jump. So Chip and Max, the other Badger goalie, trudged into the locker room to get the rest of their stuff. Max was muttering something to Chip, who just shrugged.

Cam, watching the goalies walk through the locker door, said, "There go two unhappy guys."

"Maybe it's good for them to work more in full pads," Brent said. "Coach Seabrook is supposed to be a defense specialist. He must have his reasons. Maybe they'll get in better shape this way."

Cam stared at his friend. Then he laughed. "Wow! You really *are* trying to give the guy a break."

Brent didn't see what was so funny. "I said I would, didn't I?"

5

Coach Maxwell gathered the centers and wings together after the break. "We're going to start with something that should be fun," he said. "This drill is designed to help with your puck-handling and maneuvering. Let's have five of you guys — Ted, Gavin, Sandy, Brent, and . . . okay, you, too, Mick. Each of you get a puck from the bench and get into the face-off circle, here."

Pucks in hand, Brent and his four teammates stood in the circle, which was thirty feet across.

The coach nodded. "Put your pucks down in front of you. When I blow my whistle, you're going to try to stay inside the circle, moving your puck with your stick. You also have to try to poke the other guys' pucks out of the circle. If your puck goes out of the circle, you have to bring it back into the circle.

"*But*, before you can come back into the circle, you have to go around the outside of the circle, twice. When only one of you is left in the circle with his puck, he's the winner. Any questions? Okay, after we have a winner, five more of you will give it a try."

Coach Maxwell blew his whistle, and the game started.

It wasn't easy, Brent soon realized. He had to keep watching for poke checks from the other players, while moving his own puck and watching for opportunities to slap an opponent's puck out of the circle. Just as he tried to jab Sandy's puck away, Gavin got Brent's puck and knocked it loose. Brent chased it down and raced around the circle twice, as fast as he could. When he got back, there were still three other players inside.

Brent was quick to see why this game was a great drill. It was really good for sharpening reflexes, and it forced you to make lightning maneuvers on your skates and use your stick as rapidly as you could.

He was really breathing hard a minute later, when the only ones left in the face-off circle were he and Ted. His stick had begun to feel like lead in his hands when he lunged forward to try to poke away Ted's puck. But Ted made a quick backhanded move to keep his puck out of Brent's reach and shoved his own stick forward at Brent's puck before Brent could recover. Brent's puck skittered out of the circle just before Sandy got back in, leaving Ted all by himself, the winner.

"Very good!" Coach Maxwell said. "Wrists and arms feeling tired?"

Brent grinned. His wrists were aching. He didn't often give them such a concentrated workout.

"I'll show you guys a couple of exercises you can use to build up those arms with weights," the coach said. "It'd be good for you to build yourselves up a little. All right, let's have the rest of you guys in the circle."

While the second group did the drill, Brent looked down the ice to see what Coach Seabrook was doing with the defensemen. At the moment, he had them practicing hip checks. A player would move forward dribbling a puck, as if he were on an offensive drive. A second man, playing the defender, would face him, bend down, turn sideways to the line of the first player's advance, and throw a hip into the guy's hips and thighs. This maneuver, if done right, would separate the offensive player from the puck, maybe even knock him off-stride and out of the play for the moment.

As Brent watched, Cam threw a hip check at a defender named Arno, a quiet kid who Brent didn't know too well. Cam did the move well, and sure enough, as he hit Arno at hip level, the puck skidded away from Arno's stick. It looked fine to Brent, but Coach Seabrook shook his head and beckoned to Cam, who came over, looking puzzled. The coach spoke quietly to Cam, gesturing and squatting as he talked. Cam nodded, and the coach signaled for the two players to go again.

This time, Cam hit Arno lower, at about the knees, and Arno sprawled on the ice. Brent wasn't close enough to be sure and hadn't had a clear-enough view, but it looked to him like Cam might have drawn a penalty for such a move, maybe even a major misconduct. But Coach Seabrook nodded and clapped his hands in approval. Cam started over to help Arno back up, but the coach held out a hand to stop him, shaking his head. Clearly, he didn't want Cam to help his opponent up. Arno got to his feet on his own.

Brent turned back toward the drill that Coach Maxwell was running. He found it hard to concentrate on what he was watching. Had Coach Seabrook been showing the Badger defensemen a dirty play? He couldn't be sure, and he didn't want to be unfair and make a hasty judgment. For all he knew, there was nothing illegal about what he'd seen. He decided he'd talk to Lee about it that evening. Lee would be able to give him good advice.

A whistle from Coach Maxwell took Brent's mind away from his troubling thoughts about Coach Seabrook.

"Good work, guys," the coach said. "Now, let's work on face-offs." Face-offs are crucial in hockey; they begin every period and start play after a team scores, after a time-out, or when the action is stopped for a penalty. A player from each team, usually the center, faces an opponent in the middle of the circle, with the other players (except the goalie) just outside the circle. When the teams are set, a linesman drops the puck on the face-off spot, between the two centers, who must have their sticks resting on the ice when the puck is dropped. Each center tries to get the puck out to one of his wings or, if the face-off is near his goal, to a defenseman behind him.

The coach placed two centers, Ted and Gavin, on either side of the face-off spot. He pointed to Brent and Sandy. "You two are Ted's wings for this drill.

Barry and Gil are on Gavin's team. I'll drop the puck. Let's see which team can control the puck off a face-off. Ready?"

The players lined up as directed. The coach made sure that the centers had their sticks on the ice and that the wings were outside the circle, then he dropped the puck between them. Ted knocked Gavin's stick away and scooped the puck back to Brent, who skated toward the boards, away from Gil, before passing to Sandy.

The coach whistled to stop play. "Good move, Ted. Gavin, before I dropped the puck, I noticed that you were watching Ted. On a face-off, keep your eyes on the linesman. That's the way to know the instant the puck is dropped. And you'll control your stick better if you slide your bottom hand down toward the blade before the puck is dropped. That way, you'll have more power to move the stick. Let's try it again."

The group worked on face-off techniques for a while. Finally, Coach Maxwell said, "Good work! When the defensemen join us, we'll work on face-off plays with them. For now, I want to —"

He was interrupted by loud voices from the other end of the rink. Several players were milling around.

Coach Seabrook was trying to get into the middle of the bunch, where something was going on. It was impossible for Brent to see what was happening. Coach Maxwell immediately headed across the ice, followed by the offensive players.

Brent saw Cam and Chip standing on the edge of the crowd. They both looked unhappy and tense. Coach Maxwell moved between them and blew his whistle sharply. "What's going on here?" he called. "Whatever it is, cut it out! *Now!*"

Players moved away from whoever was in the middle. Coach Seabrook, red-faced, came toward Coach Maxwell. He smiled and shook his head. "It's nothing, really," he said. "A couple of the boys just got a little . . . excited, that's all. The kind of thing that sometimes happens when boys are playing, I'm sure you've seen it all before . . ."

Now Brent saw that Vic and Arno were wrestling with each other on the ice. Brent knew Arno to be a quiet boy who never lost his cool. It would have taken something major for him to get into it like this, especially with a strong guy like Vic.

"Both of you, on your feet," snapped Coach Maxwell. He wasn't yelling, but his face showed that he was seriously angry. He turned to Coach Seabrook. "No, I *haven't* seen it all before," he said. "I'm not used to seeing two teammates behaving like this. What started it?"

Coach Seabrook said, "Well, it was really nothing much, just the kind of collision that can happen in a sport like hockey. The boys just got tangled up, that's all. Then things sort of got a little heated. But no harm done."

He put a hand on Arno's shoulder, but the boy shook it off.

"This guy tried to knock me into the boards," Arno yelled. "He did it on purpose!"

Brent looked at Vic, whose face looked like it was carved out of stone. He didn't say yes or no, didn't look angry or upset.

Coach Seabrook smiled. "I think you're making more of this than it really is, son. You're not hurt, are you?"

Arno looked ready to yell some more, but Coach Maxwell said, "Arno, are you all right? How do you feel?"

"Okay, I guess," he said. "But what he did, that was really rotten."

"What happened, Vic?" asked Coach Maxwell. "I'd like to hear from you."

Vic shrugged. "I gave him a body check, that's all. And I guess it was a little close to the boards. So he, like, gets all bent out of shape, like I hit him with a baseball bat or something. He didn't get hurt, it looks like."

He said something else, under his breath, that nobody could hear.

Coach Maxwell frowned. "I missed that last bit, Vic. What did you say?"

Vic looked at his father, then at Coach Maxwell. "Nothing. Only . . . hey, sometimes people run into each other in hockey. Right? That's why we wear all the pads."

Vic's father licked his lips. "Things like this are going to happen, Coach. And the main thing is, nobody got hurt. Isn't that right?"

Coach Maxwell looked at the two boys who had been fighting. He said, "Arno, you sure you're okay?"

Arno nodded. "Yeah, I guess."

Coach Maxwell said, "Let's take a little break, so everyone can settle down. Coach, let's talk for a bit."

As the two men walked to where they wouldn't be overheard, Brent skated up to Cam.

"What was *that* all about?"

"I don't know," Cam replied. "I wasn't watching. Coach was showing a new way of making body checks, and I was adjusting my pads. I hear this *crash* and next thing, Arno's yelling stuff like, 'Are you *crazy*, what are you doing?' And they're down on the ice, getting into it."

"What kind of stuff was Coach Seabrook teaching?"

"What do you mean, what kind of stuff?" Cam was annoyed. "Defensive stuff. Different checks, stick-handling, you know. *Stuff*. What are you getting at?"

Brent knew that Cam would be angry, and he didn't want that, but he had to say what was on his mind.

"Arno never goes ballistic. He's too easygoing."

"Yeah, so?" Cam wouldn't look at Brent. "So he got mad. Big deal. Vic's right, it wasn't anything to go crazy about."

Brent said, "I watched you put a nice check on Arno a few minutes ago. You totally took him out of the action."

Cam said, "Anything wrong with that?"

"No way! It was perfect. Your check was hard, but it was clean. Then Coach Seabrook had you do it again. The second time, you hit Arno at the knees. Knocked him down."

Cam looked Brent in the eye. "Right. That's how the game is supposed to be played. You'll see a lot more of that from now on."

Brent felt a sinking feeling in his stomach. "We will, huh?"

Cam leaned forward. He clearly wanted Brent to see the wisdom of what he said. "I know you don't like it. But think about Coach Seabrook's point of view. He makes a lot of sense. I like Coach Maxwell. He's a nice guy who knows a lot about hockey.

"But he doesn't know about how to *win*. We're not going to be a winning team, playing his way. Oh, we'll beat weak teams, but good teams will beat *us*. We don't play to win. It's like, under Coach Maxwell, winning doesn't matter. Now, we have the chance to turn things around. Don't you get it?"

Brent said, "Yeah, I get it. Winning is what matters. No matter how you do it. Great."

"You make it sound like winning is a terrible thing,"

said Cam. "What's the matter with winning? Why else do we keep score?"

"I want to win, too," insisted Brent. "It's just that . . . there are things I won't do to win. I thought you felt the same way."

"What do you mean?" Cam asked. The look he gave Brent wasn't friendly. Brent hadn't wanted this conversation, but now that he was in it, he figured he might as well finish it, whatever happened.

"Here's what I mean," he said, meeting Cam's eyes with a steady stare of his own. "Say you knew you could get away with an illegal play, like tripping an opponent on a breakaway to stop a goal. The officials wouldn't see you do it. Would you commit the foul?

Cam's mouth opened, but he didn't speak for a moment. Finally, he said, "That's a dumb question!"

Brent shook his head. "No, it's not. It's a *tough* question. Would you cheat to win, if you knew you could get away with it? It's not a dumb question at all. You got an answer?"

"It *is* a dumb question, and I don't want to answer." Cam turned away and then wheeled around. "Wake up, Brent. *Grow* up! You play sports to *win.* End of discussion!" He skated off angrily.

A few other players stared curiously at Cam and Brent. They had heard only the end of the argument and didn't know what had happened. Brent wanted to go after Cam and try to put things right, but realized that he should just wait awhile. Maybe he hadn't handled this right, but Cam would chill out, and they'd be friends again.

He hoped.

6

Brent wished that he had heard what had gone down between the two coaches, but it wasn't possible. It didn't look like they had argued. And when they returned to the team, they seemed friendly enough.

Coach Maxwell called the Badgers together. "Guys, it'll happen now and then that, when you play hockey, there'll be collisions and bruises. Once in a while, tempers will flare up. But I don't want to see teammates fighting. Not ever. Let's get back to work and put the bad feeling behind us, okay?"

Arno skated over to Vic. "Sorry I got hot, there." He stuck out his hand.

Vic nodded and shook hands. But he didn't say a word. His father grinned and said, "Way to be, guys! We're a team. All right!"

It seemed to Brent that Arno still looked unhappy.

51

Brent also noticed two other defensemen whispering to each other. One of them jerked a thumb toward Vic, and the other one scowled. What was going on?

"I want to spend the rest of the practice on power plays and penalty killing," said Coach Maxwell. "For starters, let's have Sandy, Brent, Ted, Arno, and Burt on offense. For penalty killers, how about Cam, Vic, Gavin, and Barry. Chip, you'll be in goal. You already have your pads on, so we don't need to wait."

Brent had forgotten to wonder why Coach Seabrook had told the goalies to put on all their gear. He decided he'd ask Chip or Max about that when he had the chance.

But now he had to focus on practice. Coach Maxwell gathered the power-play group together, and Coach Seabrook took the penalty killers aside to give them a strategy.

"This is a little different from the umbrella we worked on earlier," said Coach Maxwell, holding a clipboard and a marking pen. "Sandy, you're the center. Start in the middle, just in front of the blue line. Burt, Arno, get here . . . and here, ten feet from the boards on the left and the right, and ten feet deeper toward the goal than Sandy. Ted and Brent, you start fifteen feet from the goal and just wide of the cage on either side.

"Sandy, you're the guy who gets things going here. You pass to either Burt or Arno. Whoever gets the puck looks to see whether the defense commits itself. If defenders move toward you," said the coach, drawing lines with his pen, "you can pass deep to Ted or Brent. They might shoot, pass it back out, or send it behind the cage to the other wing. See? The idea is to use quick passing to try to open up a hole in the defense and get a good shot on goal. Any questions? Good. Remember, it's a two-minute penalty. You don't have to rush to get off a shot. Let the play develop and don't waste the opportunity."

As the power-play unit got set, Brent looked at the defensive setup. The four defensemen had formed a diamond with Cam at the point, facing Sandy. Vic and Barry flanked him, back a few yards on either side. Gavin was deep, playing just in front of the cage, five feet from Chip. Coach Maxwell placed the puck at Sandy's feet, stepped back, and blew the whistle.

Cam charged at the startled Sandy, who hadn't expected it. Hastily, he slapped a pass to Brent on his left. Brent took it on his stick and held it a moment, eyeing Vic, the closest defender. Cam swerved away from Sandy and went toward Brent. At the same time, Vic moved in as well. The two obviously hoped to trap Brent before he could get rid of the puck. But Brent skated down the ice along the boards, away from Cam. Seeing Burt open, not far from the goalmouth, he fired the puck at him.

As Brent took the pass, Chip shifted to face him. Arno, on offense, moved in front of the goal, and Gavin slid over to cover him. Burt wheeled around and passed across the ice to Ted near the right-side boards. Barry raced toward Ted, who feinted as if he were going to pass back to Sandy, hoping to draw Barry out of position and possibly open up a shooting lane.

But Barry didn't bother with the feint. He kept going straight at Ted, who moved to his right, closer to the boards, hoping to swing around Barry and get deeper and closer to the crease — the area immediately in front of the goalmouth. At the same time, Arno turned and moved away from the goal so Ted could get him the puck.

Seeing Arno skate toward him, Ted flicked a backhand pass down the ice to Arno, figuring that Barry would turn and move back to help Gavin protect the crease. From his position across the ice, Brent watched the action, assuming, as Ted did, that Barry would back up to help prevent any shots.

But Barry ignored the puck and zeroed in on Ted, who had turned to watch Arno take his pass. He was ready to move in behind Arno and be in position if Arno chose to pass back out. Concentrating on the play near the goal, Ted was paying no attention to Barry. Head down, arms pumping, Barry lowered his shoulder and slammed into Ted.

Ted slumped to the ice and didn't move. Coach Maxwell blew his whistle and raced over. Ted slowly got to his knees and shook his head. He tried to get to his feet.

Brent couldn't believe what he had just seen. Barry, an easygoing guy, never lost his temper. He had rarely drawn a penalty, and when he did, it wasn't done on purpose. Now, he watched Coach Maxwell take Ted's arm and help him off the ice to a bench. After Ted sat down, the coach had Ted remove his helmet and squatted in front of the dazed boy. He looked at him and spoke to him quietly. Ted nodded, and Brent heard him say, "I'm okay. It just knocked the wind out of me, that's all."

Brent was sure that Ted was only stunned. He saw that Barry looked a little stunned himself, standing near the boards, as if he could not understand or believe what he had done. Vic skated over to Barry and draped an arm around his shoulders, saying something to him. Brent couldn't hear what he said, but he saw Barry wheel around and look at Vic with surprise.

"*No!* You're wrong!" Barry said. "I *didn't* want that." He shook off Vic's arm and glared. Vic shrugged and skated over to Cam.

After making sure that Ted was all right, Coach Maxwell went back on the ice and skated over to Barry. The rest of the Badgers stood around quietly.

When the coach spoke, he didn't raise his voice. "If this had been a game, and I was an official, I'd have called that a major penalty for charging. A strict official might even make it a misconduct penalty, which would mean ten minutes in the penalty box. Personally, I'd make it only five, because Ted wasn't badly hurt — luckily.

"But, whether it's a major or a misconduct, it's bad

news — for several reasons. First, that's a way for players to get seriously hurt. Second, it's bad sportsmanship. Third —"

"But he was only —" Vic started to say.

Coach Maxwell turned and stared at Vic, who stopped immediately.

"Third," the coach went on, as though nobody had said a word, "it gives the other team a long power play and a very good chance at a goal. Any one of these is reason enough not to do it. But all three of them together . . ." — He paused and shook his head — "I don't want to see that kind of thing, in practice or games. Vic, was there something you wanted to say?"

"Uh, well . . . it was just a body check, what he did," said Vic. "I mean, that's the way it looked to me, anyway."

"Number one, Ted didn't have the puck when he was hit. Number two, his back was to the player who hit him. That makes it a serious foul, not just a body check. If you want to be sure, see the rule book. Coach Seabrook, anything to add?"

The other coach cleared his throat and said, "Uh, no, I think you said it all. What happened was . . . very unfortunate. Now I'm sure that Billy didn't mean to —"

"His name is Barry," said Coach Maxwell.

"Right, of course . . . *Barry* didn't mean to do what he did, especially in practice, to a teammate. But, to look on the bright side, I'll just point out that, uh, the other player, uh . . ."

"Ted," Coach Maxwell said.

"Thanks . . . *Ted* seems fine, and, boys, you can learn a couple of valuable lessons from what just happened. First, you have to be alert at all times when you're on the ice, and second . . . well, I guess the second thing is, don't do anything that would put your team at a disadvantage, like being caught in a major-penalty situation. I guess that's all I have to say. Thank you, Coach."

Coach Maxwell didn't say anything for a few seconds. Then he sighed and looked around. "Let's call it a day. We have two more practices before we play the Cyclones, and they always are tough competition, so let's be ready to work hard tomorrow. Now let's stow the gear."

The coaches and players put away the cones, cages, and other equipment. On the way to the locker room, Brent caught up with Chip.

"Hey," Chip said, looking and sounding depressed. "What's up?"

"I was wondering," Brent said, "how come Coach Seabrook had you and Max in full pads today?"

Chip started to answer, then stopped and looked around as if to make sure he wouldn't be overheard. He spoke in a whisper. "He talked to Max and me about how to use our blockers and catching gloves and stuff to . . . well . . . sort of . . . shove people away or knock them off balance when they are in the crease. Like when there's a bunch of players in front and the ref and the linesmen's views are blocked . . . that kind of thing."

Brent whistled. "Sounds like dirty playing to me."

Chip shrugged. He looked even more depressed. "Yeah, I said that, but the coach says that's how the game is played, that that's how they separate the winners from the losers, so we better get used to it. I mean . . . *I* don't know. I guess he knows what he's talking about."

Brent couldn't believe what he was hearing. "And what Barry just did to Ted . . . is that the kind of stuff Coach Seabrook wants us to do, too? Is that why it happened?"

Chips eyes grew wide. "*That?* Oh, no."

Brent felt a little better. "I hope not."

"No, you're not supposed to do it right in the open where a linesman can see you. You do it only when you're sure you won't get caught," said Chip. "Barry totally messed up. Well, I better get these pads off. See you."

Brent watched Chip trudge into the locker room. He didn't know what to think. The kind of hockey that Coach Seabrook was teaching went against everything he believed — and not only about sports but life in general. Rules were there to be followed. He was certain of that.

But then a scary thought came to him.

Could it be that Coach Seabrook was *right*? That what made some players winners and others losers was that the winners knew when to cheat and get away with it? Maybe that was what it was all about, and Coach Maxwell had it wrong. Maybe Lee was wrong too . . . after all, Lee might be a few years older than Brent, but he was basically still a kid himself.

Brent wished he could be sure.

And he wondered, too, if the way Coach Seabrook taught hockey was the way it was supposed to be played. If so, could he play that way?

Did he even *want* to?

7

As Brent changed into his street clothes, he noticed that the locker room was unusually quiet. There were some guys talking in low voices, while others — like himself — just dressed without a word.

He left the locker room with his equipment bag, then remembered unhappily that he was going to share a ride home with Cam, as he did on most days. Normally he looked forward to it, but not today.

Cam was already outside, and when he saw Brent, he turned away.

"Do me a favor," he said before Brent could say a word. "Don't start with that stuff. I'm not in the mood."

"I didn't say anything," Brent replied. "If you don't want to talk, well, okay."

Cam wheeled around. He looked upset. "You know

61

what I mean!" he snapped. "Don't start with that stuff about how terrible it is that the Badgers are going to be playing a different kind of hockey now. If you don't like it, that's your problem."

Brent found it hard to speak. "You don't mind what happened to Ted? That's all right to you?"

"*What* happened to Ted? He got knocked down, that's all. He didn't get hurt, did he? No, he didn't! Next time, he'll be looking for the other guy, and maybe he'll learn to play harder, too."

Brent shook his head, feeling very depressed. "And Barry will learn that you can play dirty, just so you don't get caught."

Cam rolled his eyes. "It's about time we got someone in here who knows how the game is really played! Last year the Cyclones whipped us, but this year maybe we'll have a couple of surprises waiting for them. I think we'll beat them if we play to win, and Coach Seabrook knows about playing to win. Wake up, dude! Join the real world!"

Brent said, "You know, you're right. We better not talk anymore. If that's what the real world is all about, maybe I'd rather stay out of it."

Cam shrugged. "Suit yourself."

The two boys didn't say anything more until Mrs. Mullen showed up a few minutes later. They still hadn't spoken when she dropped Cam off at his house.

"Thanks, Mrs. M.," Cam said as he pulled his equipment out of the car and slammed the door behind him.

Brent's mother looked at her son. "What's the matter?" she asked.

"Nothing," Brent muttered. "I don't know. It's . . . nothing."

Mrs. Mullen sighed. "I can see that it's not 'nothing,' but if you won't talk, I'm not going to pry. I just hate to see two good friends acting like this."

Brent's bad mood lasted through dinner. The family saw that something was wrong but didn't try to get him to open up. As he picked at his food, Brent saw a look pass between his father and Lee. Sure enough, as soon as dinner was over, Lee said, "Got a minute?"

"Yeah, I guess."

The brothers went to the basement, which was fixed up as a den. Brent sprawled on a couch, and Lee sat on a chair across from him.

"What's up?" asked Lee. "Something wrong between you and Cam?"

Brent sighed. "I guess."

Lee nodded. "You were worried about a couple of things the other day. How's it going with the new coach and the new kid?"

"Terrible!" Brent said. "I think this Coach Seabrook is bad news. I don't know, maybe he's right and Coach Maxwell is wrong, and *I'm* wrong and *you're* wrong. I just don't know what to do. But Cam thinks the new coach is great and that he'll make us into a winning team, and maybe he will, but if that's how you get to be a winning team then I don't think I want to be on a winning team —"

"Hey, slow down," Lee said. "Let's hear what this guy is doing. Take your time."

Brent described what had happened since the new coach had started with the team. He talked about Barry and Ted, and then he told him what Chip had said about Coach Seabrook teaching the Badgers to get away with illegal plays. As Brent talked, Lee's frown grew deeper.

"Anyway," Brent went on, "the thing with Cam happened because Cam thinks Coach Seabrook is *right*. And he thinks that that's how we should play. So I said that I didn't like it, and he got all uptight."

"Uh-huh," Lee said. "I can see how that would bother you. It would get to me, too."

"The thing of it is," Brent said, staring at his brother, "I don't know, maybe that *is* how to play the game. I just don't know!"

"Don't even *think* that." Lee stood up and began walking back and forth across the room. "If this new guy *is* right and Coach Maxwell is wrong, then the guys I play with and our coach are wrong, too. And that doesn't just go for hockey, either."

The older boy stood still for a moment thinking. He sat back down and looked hard at Brent. "Are you absolutely sure about what you're telling me? I mean, there's no way you could have misunderstood, is there?"

Brent shook his head. "No way! I saw Vic commit fouls, I saw Barry slam into Ted, and I heard what Chip said. *And* I talked to Cam. The thing is, what should I do now?"

Before Lee could reply, footsteps sounded on the stairs, and Mr. Mullen appeared on the landing. "I don't want to interrupt, but is there something I should know about?"

"Yeah, there is," said Lee. "This Coach Seabrook is

bad news. Brent says he's teaching guys to cheat and play rough. Somebody's going to get hurt, and I think he should be stopped!"

Mr. Mullen was a hockey fan who'd played in his younger days. He said, "That's a serious accusation. If it's true —"

Brent jumped in, anxious to convince his father. "It *is!*"

Mr. Mullen sat on the couch. "Mind going through it again, for my benefit?"

Brent repeated what he'd told Lee.

"See?" demanded the older boy. "This guy has to be stopped! They shouldn't let him coach! And his kid sounds like bad news, too."

"Brent, I don't doubt your word," Mr. Mullen said, "but I'd like to know a little more before I do anything. It's important that we don't act too hastily. First, I want to call Coach Maxwell and hear what he says about all this. If he's not happy with the new coach, then I may call some other parents and discuss this with them. But I need Coach Maxwell's input first. Till then, keep this to yourselves. No talking to your friends or anyone else, understood?"

Lee nodded. Brent looked unsure. "What do I do?

We have practice tomorrow. What if Coach Seabrook wants me to do something I don't like?

"Say, 'No way!'" Lee said.

Mr. Mullen smiled. "I wouldn't put it that way, but if anyone asks you to do something that you don't feel right about, don't do it. You can simply say that you believe in playing by the rules of the game, and that's what you're going to do. I can't believe that Coach Maxwell would stand for anything else. Don't yell, don't be rude. Just tell them that you plan to stick to the rules. All right?"

Brent felt a little better. "Yeah."

"Good," said Mr. Mullen. "I'll phone Coach Maxwell tonight. And, Brent, I'm pleased that you know the difference between right and wrong. It makes me feel we did a good job raising you."

Brent was happy to hear his father say that. He only wished that doing the right thing was easier to live with.

8

Brent was uneasy about practice the whole next day. His father had met with Coach Maxwell that morning, and they'd had their chat. But Brent didn't have a clue about what had been said. He had avoided Cam during school, and Cam probably had been just as pleased not to run into him.

When Brent arrived at the rink, Coach Maxwell was standing by himself outside. He saw Brent and walked over.

"I was hoping to catch you before we started today," he said. He pointed to a bench under a tree in a little park across the street. "Let's sit down and talk for a few minutes."

Brent nodded. He suddenly felt terribly nervous. His throat was dry, and he wasn't sure he'd be able to talk. It suddenly struck him that he'd done a terrible thing: he'd complained about one of his coaches. Maybe he'd even get kicked off the team!

Once he and the coach were sitting on the bench, Coach Maxwell said, "I had a long conversation with your dad this morning. He told me about what was on your mind."

Brent stammered, "I know I shouldn't go behind a coach's back, but I —"

"That's all right," said the coach, waving off Brent's apology. "I know that what happened yesterday bothered you, and I understand it. It left some other boys feeling the same way. Just between us, your father wasn't the only parent I heard from afterward."

Brent was startled, he had thought that he'd been the only one to be worried. "Who else?" he asked.

Coach Maxwell shook his head. "I can't discuss that, and I'd appreciate your not mentioning what I just told you. I'm not sure I should have even said that much, but I felt you needed to realize that you weren't alone.

"There's something else I want you to understand, too. I've coached the Badgers for a long time. It's my team, and it'll keep being my team, and I'm going to keep being the same kind of coach I've always been. A won-lost record has never been my top priority. Working with young athletes like you, a coach's biggest responsibility is seeing that they respect the rules and practice sportsmanship. So don't worry about us turning into a bunch of bad guys. It's not going to happen."

Brent felt somewhat better but not completely. "But what about the new coach?"

Coach Maxwell said, "That's for me to take care of. All you need to remember is that I'm the head coach, and I set the policy. Okay?"

"Okay," Brent replied, hoping it was so.

The coach grinned. "In that case, let's get to work. We've got a lot to do."

From the moment he walked into the locker room, it was clear to Brent that there was some tension between the players. During the stretches, it seemed like boys got into groups that weren't the same as the old groups. For example, Brent and Cam would have been staying together, but now Brent was with a bunch of players that included Ted, Sandy, and Arno. Cam hung with Vic, Gavin, and Burt.

Also, there wasn't much friendly exchange and joking between the groups, which had always been a habit in the locker room.

During warm-ups, Brent saw the two coaches talking together just off the ice. It didn't seem like a casual conversation, as far as Brent could tell. He reminded himself of what Coach Maxwell had said: he was the *head* coach and Coach Seabrook was the assistant.

During the skatearound, Brent saw Sandy stumble and almost fall. He recovered his balance and looked around angrily. He saw Cam and Vic skating together, not far away, and glared at them.

"That's not funny," he said. "Cut it out!"

"Cut *what* out?" Cam said while Vic snickered. "Don't blame me just because you can't stay on your feet!"

Sandy muttered something under his breath while Cam and Vic grinned at each other. Sandy said something to Ted, who nodded and gave Cam a dirty look, which Cam returned. Brent wondered whether Coach Maxwell was aware of what was going on. He hoped so and wished that the coach would do something about it.

Once the skatearound was finished, Coach Maxwell called the team together. He stood next to Coach Seabrook in front of the players, looking at each boy in turn, saying nothing. It seemed like endless time passed before he finally spoke.

"Each year, when the Badgers have their first meeting,

71

I give a speech. Basically, it's the same speech every time. I say that one of my jobs as coach is to teach techniques and skills that make good hockey players. Another job is to tell kids about strategies and tactics you'll need to compete.

"The third, and most important job — to me — is to show you what it is to be part of a *team* and get you to see how a team sport can help you go from being kids to young men. As you grow up, you'll find that you're part of many groups: not just teams but clubs, classes, work crews, families, and so on. I really believe that team sports can help you prepare to work with those different groups later in life. For most of what you'll do as adults, winning — being number one — isn't what matters.

"Chances are that none of you will be a pro athlete. Most of you won't want to be. You'll get jobs, have careers, families, and so forth. And I really urge you *not* to make being number one your yardstick for measuring success or failure. There's very little room for number ones, and if you see anything less as a failure, then you may wind up leading an unhappy life. The fact is that you can be happy and satisfied with your life even if you're *not number one*. And when you play a sport, win or lose, if you do your best, you should enjoy it. That's what it should be about.

"As long as I'm coaching this team, I want you to see yourselves as a team. To play together, respect each other, and finish each game and each season feeling that you gave it your best shot, and that this made for a successful season. I hope you all see it that way. I don't want to see any fighting, arguing, or bad feelings among team members.

"Okay, enough. Let's go to work."

Brent loved what the coach had said. He and several other players nodded, and there was some hand clapping afterward. But some of the Badgers, he noticed, didn't react at all. Of course, silence was also a reaction.

Coach Seabrook cleared his throat. "Uh, can I add something?"

"Of course," said Coach Maxwell.

The other coach stepped forward and smiled. Brent didn't know why this man's smile made him uncomfortable, but it did.

"I applaud what Coach Maxwell had to say," said the other man. "You're lucky to have him here. I can't think of a single thing to disagree with in his talk.

"The only thing I'd like to add is that 'winning' isn't

a terrible thing. Sure, when you don't win a game, it shouldn't make you feel ashamed. But, personally, I always felt better when I won than when I lost. I think this team can win. And that's what I'm here to help you boys do. That's why Coach Maxwell and I work together so well. I'll be concentrating on one thing while he's working on another. Between us, we'll not only make you a team, but we'll make you a *winning* team!"

"All *right!*" Cam said, clapping. He and Vic gave each other high-fives, and a few other players nodded, clapped, and looked excited by what Coach Seabrook said.

Brent sat silently. He couldn't be sure, but he guessed that Coach Maxwell didn't like it either. Coach Seabrook hadn't come out and said that he thought the other coach was wrong, but it was clear that he felt that way — and so it seemed did some of Brent's teammates.

Coach Maxwell said, "Okay, let's start with a few drills. We'll begin by working on our backhand passing and shooting."

He arranged two nets across from each other midway between the blue line and the end boards. "Chip, you take the goal on this side," he said, pointing to one of the nets. "Max, get in goal on the other side. The point of this drill is to use your backhand. You'll use only your backhand to pass and to shoot. We'll play three-on-three. We may as well practice 'changing on the fly' while we do this drill."

Ice hockey demands such all-out energy that even professionals can only go full-strength for a minute or so. This often means that players must substitute for teammates without stopping the action, which is called changing on the fly. A group of players hustles off the ice to the bench while fresh players swing over the boards into the game. It has to be done with lightning speed. If the subs go in too slowly, the opposing team may get a chance at an easy goal. But if the subs get on before the other players are off, an official will penalize the team for having too many men on the ice, and someone will spend two minutes in the penalty box. Teams practice changing on the fly to get the timing down perfectly.

Coach Maxwell split the Badgers into two squads. The squad members who didn't start the drill sat on the sidelines, ready to come in whenever the coach blew his whistle. Coach Seabrook was in charge of one squad, and Coach Maxwell took the other one himself.

"You guys on the bench, when the coach calls your name, be ready to change on the fly. Remember, all your passes and shots have to be backhand for this drill. Ready?"

The coach gave the puck to Brent's squad to start, and then he blew the whistle. Brent was on the ice with Ted and Arno. Their goalie was Chip. Opposing them were Cam, Gavin, and Sandy, with Max in goal. Ted sent a pass to Brent, but his backhand was weak, and Gavin intercepted. He had a better backhand and shot a pass over to Cam, who advanced on Chip. Chip came out to cut down Cam's shooting angle, but Cam passed to his right, where Sandy received it. Sandy passed back to Gavin, but . . .

The whistle stopped play. "*Backhand* passes only," Coach Maxwell said.

"Sorry, I just forgot," said Sandy, looking sheepish.

"That's okay, pick it up from there," said the coach. Sandy passed to Cam, who tried a backhand shot that Chip stopped with a glove save. He dropped the puck and backhanded it to Arno. Arno saw Brent headed toward the other goal and passed to him. Noticing Ted coming up alongside, Brent got him the puck, and Ted fired a shot that skimmed under Max's stick for a goal.

"Real nice save, Max," muttered Cam. Brent heard Cam, but he thought that nobody else had. Still, he was upset by Cam's comment. What was going on with his old friend?

Max hooked the puck out of the net and flipped it to Cam. But before a play could get going, the whistle sounded.

"Change!" yelled Coach Maxwell to his squad. Brent, Arno, and Ted raced for the sidelines and, as they scrambled over the boards, their three replacements moved in hurriedly to keep the other squad from scoring. But Coach Seabrook blew his whistle before a scoring attempt could be made.

"Change!" he called out. Cam, Sandy, and Gavin skated hard for the boards as three substitutes jumped to the ice . . . a little before the first three had gotten off.

Brent poked Arno in the side. "Those guys got on too soon. That was a foul!"

Arno laughed, but there wasn't any pleasure in the sound. "Are you surprised?" he asked. "The new coach must have told them to jump the gun a little. That's another way to be winners, didn't you know?"

Brent looked at Arno in surprise. It wasn't like the

old Arno to sound so unhappy and angry. He looked at Brent and said, "Don't tell anyone yet, but I think I may quit the team. I don't need this stuff."

"Whoa." Brent basically liked Arno, and he didn't like the idea of losing him. "Don't do anything yet. Coach Maxwell won't let this happen. You have to trust him."

Arno said, "Maybe it won't be up to him. You can see that some guys *like* this thing about being winners, no matter what. And so do some of their parents."

"How do you know?" Brent asked.

"When I talked to my dad about this new coach last night, he said he'd call some other parents. He was sure that they'd be as angry as he was," Arno answered. "Later I asked what happened when he called them, but he didn't want to talk about it. Why wouldn't he talk about it if they felt like he did? I think they like the new coach."

Brent suddenly felt like he couldn't be sure of anything anymore. Somehow, he'd felt that Coach Maxwell would always be able to stay in charge, that he would find a way.

But maybe this story wouldn't have a happy ending.

9

For the moment, Brent thought, he was part of the team, and the Badgers were going to play the Cyclones in a couple of days. The Cyclones were tough, so he knew he had to try to forget everything that might distract him and focus on playing hockey.

"All right, you sharpshooters," said Coach Maxwell, "let's see how accurate your shooting really is." He skated to the side of the rink and brought back three pieces of cloth called "shooter tutors." The coach and two players used bungee cords to attach the cloths to the goals they'd used for the backhand drill and another goal at the far end of the ice. The cloths covered the goalmouths completely and were designed with five circular holes. The holes were located near the four corners of the goals, with the fifth hole in the middle, eight inches above the ice.

"You know how this goes," said Coach Maxwell. "I divide the team into three groups. Each group has a puck, and you line up. The first player passes to the one behind him, and that player has to shoot, aiming at any of the five holes. Those holes represent the best areas to score: the corners of the net and low in the middle. The group gets two points for each puck that goes through a hole. If you miss your shot, pass the puck back to the next guy in line, and he shoots right away off the pass. If you make the shot, get the puck and pass it back in the same way. The group with the most points after two minutes wins. I'll keep score for one group, Coach Seabrook will do the second, and, since we're not using a goalie, Chip can keep score for the third group. Line up!"

Brent enjoyed this drill, even though he wasn't one of the best shooters on the team. And he was relieved to have something to do that would take his mind off the problems threatening the team.

He was in the same group as Vic, who was directly in front of him. When Vic's turn came to shoot, Brent wasn't surprised to see that Vic was barely able to hit the goalmouth, let alone put the puck in one of the holes. Then he seemed to take forever getting the puck back onto his stick. Finally he managed to send a weak pass in Brent's direction.

Brent fired a shot that caught the edge of the lower left hole and tumbled into the cage for 2 points. "Good goal!" shouted Chip, who was scoring for Brent's squad.

As Brent hooked the puck out of the goal with his stick, Sandy caught his eye and called out, "Nice shot!"

Brent nodded in response and sent a pass back to Burt, who was next in line. When Brent got another shot opportunity, he aimed for the center hole but missed when his shot went high. At the end of two minutes, Coach Maxwell blew his whistle again. *"Time!"* he called. "This group has eighteen points."

"Sixteen points here," said Coach Seabrook.

"Sixteen here, too," said Chip.

"One more time, same squads," said Coach Maxwell. "Remember, when you try flip shots, get the toe of your stick right under the puck and put your wrists into it. Okay?"

He blew his whistle. Brent took a pass from Vic and tried a flip shot at the upper right hole. Remembering the coach's advice, he really gave it everything he had with his wrists — and the puck sailed completely over the net. As he raced to retrieve the puck, he heard someone snicker behind him and say, "Brilliant shot."

It was Vic.

Furious, Brent whirled around and glared at Vic, who smirked back at him.

"The clock's running, Brent," Chip said quietly. Brent took a deep breath and went to get the puck. He knew he'd almost lost it, and that would have been bad news. Instead, he flicked a pass to Burt, who fired a shot into the middle hole.

"Good one," he said as Burt went by.

"Thanks, dude. Chill out," murmured Burt.

When Brent's turn came again, Vic's pass was way off to the side. Brent lunged after the puck, got it under control, took a deep breath, and shot it into the lower right hole for 2 points. Yes! he said to himself, retrieving the rubber disk and sending it to Burt again.

When Burt got behind him in the line, he tapped Brent's shoulder. "Don't let that creep get to you," he said in a low voice. "That's just what he wants to happen."

"Yeah, I know," Brent said. "Thanks."

After the second round, Coach Maxwell clapped his hands. "The point total was up that time," he said. "Twenty-four each for two squads and twenty-two for the other one. In other words, you shot better. Way to go.

"Let's work on our bodychecking. There's a lot of hard physical contact in hockey, but we have to make sure we know the difference between clean, legal checks and the kind that send you to the penalty box."

Coach Maxwell set up a line of traffic cones between one of the blue lines and the line along the goalmouth, twenty feet from the boards. He moved the goal from its normal position so that it was midway between the line of cones and the side of the rink, and then he put another goal on the blue line, facing the first one. The result was a long, narrow playing area, twenty feet wide and sixty feet long. The players stared; this drill was new to them.

"We'll play two-on-two between these goals," the coach said. "You play for a minute and a half, then I blow the whistle and send in two new players on each side for a new matchup. The object is to score goals and to keep the opponents from scoring with legal body checks. *Legal* is the key word. No high sticks, no checks into someone's back, no elbows, and so on. Your team gets two points for each legal body check and loses two points for each illegal one. You also get a point for every goal. In this drill, solid checks count for more than goals. Coach Seabrook will keep score, and I'll officiate. Questions? Okay, Ted and Burt will start on my left, and Sandy and Cam, on my right. Sandy, Ted, get set for a face-off."

Coach Maxwell dropped the puck between Sandy and Ted. Ted's reflexes were a little quicker. He flicked the disk back to Burt, but Cam hit Burt hard with his upper body and knocked him away from the puck.

"Good check! Two points!" called Coach Maxwell. Cam got to the loose puck and swung his stick back for a shot, but before he could connect, Burt crunched him. "Good check the other way!"

A moment later, Cam came into Ted hard, but Ted had been moving away from him, so Cam ended up hitting Ted in the back, knocking him forward.

"No!" called Coach Maxwell. "In the back! Two points off, Cam."

Cam rolled his eyes and looked angry but said nothing. He knew that his hit had been illegal. A few seconds later, Burt got penalized 2 points for hitting Cam with his elbows and stick raised.

Brent had thought that there'd be lots of goals, but then he saw that the narrow playing area made scoring more difficult. Just before the ninety seconds ended, Cam managed to snap a pass to Sandy, who put the puck through the unguarded net for a 1-point goal. After the final whistle, Cam and Sandy had 9 points and Ted and Burt had 6.

Now it was Brent's turn. He was teamed with Gavin, against Vic and Gil. Brent faced off against Gil and got control of the puck. Vic came forward at him, but Brent veered sharply to his left. Vic couldn't swing around quickly enough, and Brent saw Gavin open on his left. He dropped a backhand pass to his teammate, who appeared to have an easy shot in front of him. But Gil lunged ahead, got himself between Gavin and the net, and swung his body into Gavin so that Gavin couldn't keep the puck on his stick. It was a nice check, good for 2 points.

Brent raced after the puck, but it went past the line of cones, out of bounds. The coach whistled play to a stop, got the puck back, and set up another face-off. This time, it was Gil who swept it away from Brent's stick. Just as Gil controlled the puck, Brent was jolted hard from just behind his right shoulder, and he stumbled forward.

"Two-point deduction for a block in the back!" called Coach Maxwell. "Vic, you have to watch out for those."

Brent heard Vic mutter "This is really dumb" as Vic got the loose disk and moved forward toward the net. Brent got in front of him and forced the chunky, slower boy toward the side. Vic lost the puck and hit the boards with a grunt.

"Two points!" the coach shouted. "Nice check, Brent!"

Vic swung around to face Coach Maxwell. "How come *he* gets two points and I *lose* two points?" he whined.

"You hit him from behind, and he hit you from in front. Keep playing," snapped the coach. Vic turned to look at his father, but Coach Seabrook didn't say a word. Meanwhile Brent had the puck and passed to Gavin. Gavin saw Gil coming toward him and feinted to his left. Gil tried to check Gavin, but Gavin slid by him and put a shot into the net for a point.

Ten seconds later, Brent put a hard check on Vic for 2 more points. When Coach Maxwell blew the whistle to end the drill, Brent and Gavin had 7 points to 1 point for Vic and Gil. Gil had managed to score a goal, but Vic had lost 4 points for two illegal checks.

After everyone had had a chance to try the check drill, Coach Maxwell said, "If we give away power plays to the Cyclones, it'll cost us. I saw their game last week, and their power play is really solid. So watch out for those fouls, guys. We can't afford to give them an edge like that. Everyone, take a break, and when we come back we'll have a scrimmage."

During the break, the team broke into small groups in the same way as they had before practice. Brent sat on a bench with Arno, Gavin, and Sandy. Across the rink, he saw Cam, Vic, Barry, and a couple of others having a very lively conversation. At one point, Cam looked up and saw Brent looking at him.

They stared at each other for a few seconds. Brent thought that Cam had a sad expression on his face, but they were too far apart for him to be certain. Then Cam turned away and began talking to Vic again.

Brent hoped that Cam had felt bad. Because he sure did. Hockey had been a lot more fun a couple of days ago.

10

After the break, Coach Maxwell organized an intrasquad scrimmage, six-on-six, just like in a regulation game. There were also several reserves for each squad.

"Everyone will play," the coach assured the reserves. "We'll practice some on-the-fly changes, and I'll also take breaks every few minutes to make substitutions and go over some strategies that we need to work on. And I want to thank our volunteer officials for the day. Mr. Jeffords teaches physical education at the high school, and he'll be our referee. And Mr. Wallace, our linesman, has worked as a hockey official for years. They were nice enough to give us some of their time this afternoon.

"These men will call the scrimmage just like a game. Players will be called for penalties when they occur. If that happens, the player will have to leave the ice, just like in a game. And we'll work on power plays and penalty killing. Here's how I'm splitting the team."

The coach read off the names of the players on each squad. Among the Badgers playing with Brent were Cam, Gavin, Sandy, Arno, and Chip, their goalie. Coach Maxwell would be in charge of this group. Vic, Ted, Barry, Gil, and Max, the other Badger goalie, were among the players on the other squad, which would be under Coach Seabrook.

The two squads gathered with their coaches for a quick huddle. Coach Maxwell said, "Play hard, just like this was a game. I won't let you burn yourselves out; I'll substitute and call plenty of time-outs. Gavin, you're my starting center. Brent and Sandy will be the wings. The starting defensemen are Cam and Arno, and Chip . . . guess you know where you'll be."

Chip, who was wearing all his pads and carrying his mask, grinned. "Guess so."

"We'll play twenty minutes, like a regular period, except we'll have more time-outs than the one that the rules allow in a period," the coach continued. "Anyone have any questions before we start?"

"I have one," said Cam. "You said we should play like this was a game, right?"

"Absolutely," Coach Maxwell said. "Don't hold anything back."

"So, we're supposed to play to win?" asked Cam.

Brent turned to look at Cam. Cam was staring at the coach.

The coach's voice remained calm. "I've always expected my team to play to win. I still do. Does that answer your question?"

"Yeah . . . I mean . . ." — Cam started to say more but stopped — "Yeah. It does."

"All right, then," said Coach Maxwell. "Let's get started."

The starters for both squads got on the ice. Gavin and Ted faced each other in the center face-off circle. Chip and Max skated to the goals at the ends of the rink. The rest of the squads lined up around the circle. Mr. Wallace crouched between the centers, holding the puck. This was always Brent's favorite moment, just before the action started. For a moment, he forgot all about the things that had been bothering him and thought only about playing.

Mr. Wallace blew a blast on his whistle and dropped the puck. Gavin's stick jabbed forward, but Ted got more power into his move and shoved Gavin's stick away, pulling the puck back and controlling it. He flipped a pass out of the circle to Cam. Brent skated out to his right. Cam saw him and sent a perfect backhand pass that Brent took in. He moved down the ice, over the red line. Out of the corner of his eye, Brent saw Gavin outskate Vic and move down the ice. Brent left a drop pass for him just as Barry veered into Brent and forced him toward the boards and away from the action. Brent eluded Barry by making a sliding stop so that Barry's momentum carried him farther down the ice. Now Brent was able to turn back toward the blue line.

In the meantime, Gavin found Sandy with a flip pass, and Sandy carried the puck over the blue line into the offensive zone. Max moved forward, blocking much of the goalmouth with his body and stick. Gil circled around Sandy from the left and tried to poke the puck away from Sandy's stick. Sandy pulled the puck back and dropped a pass to Arno, who had come up behind him.

Arno fired the puck toward the goal. Max easily deflected it away with his blocker. The puck bounced toward the boards behind the goal. Brent raced after it. So did Barry, who reached the puck first and sent it caroming around the boards and back out toward the blue line. Gil picked it up, and suddenly the game was moving in the other direction.

Brent pivoted and started back the other way, looking for a good defensive position. He noticed Cam skating backward, staying with Gil, looking for the chance to take away the puck. Suddenly, Brent spotted Barry coming up fast, with nobody on Brent's team nearby. Gil saw it, too, and sent a pass to his right, where Barry could pick it up and move it deep into scoring territory.

Brent sprinted full-speed, hoping to cut Barry off before Barry could break away for an open shot on goal.

Wham! He was no longer on his feet but smack on his belly, sliding on the ice. He rammed into the boards, hitting shoulder first.

He lay there dazed. He heard the shrill sound of a whistle, but it seemed to come from a long distance away. Then he heard a voice.

"Brent! Hey, you all right?"

It sounded like Cam, but Brent wasn't sure. He wasn't sure whether or not he was all right either. He'd try to get to his feet; then he'd know if he was okay.

"Just a second. Don't try to move yet." That voice, he knew, was Coach Maxwell's. Brent opened his eyes and realized that he was lying near the boards with the coach kneeling next to him.

"Can you hear me?" the coach asked, peering at him anxiously.

"Yeah," Brent said. "I . . . I think I'm all right. I mean, I can hear, and I can see anyway."

"Well, that's a start. Looks like you took the impact on your shoulder pads. Let's get you sitting up."

With the coach's help, Brent got into a sitting position. He noticed that the rest of the team was standing behind Coach Maxwell, staring at him, looking worried. Even Cam looked worried, which was good to see.

"What happened?" Brent asked.

"You tripped," said the coach, checking Brent for cuts or scrapes. "I think you can stand up. Come on, I'll give you a hand."

A moment later, Brent stood up. He tried moving his arms and legs and was pleased to find that everything worked and that he felt no major pains anywhere. "I'm okay."

The coach nodded. "I think you are. But I won't

take any chances. I want you on the bench for a bit. I'll bring Neil in for you for now. Come on."

With the coach by his side, Brent slowly skated off the ice. Players clapped and said things like "Way to go!" and "All *right!*"

As Brent sat down and watched the squads prepare for a face-off in the circle nearest to where the action had stopped, Brent turned to the player next to him.

"How'd I trip? Did you see?"

The player, a first-year guy named Darryl, said, "You'd almost caught Barry when he looked like he had a breakaway, and then Vic tried to catch *you* from behind, but he isn't real fast, so there was no way, you know? So, he like, reached out with his stick, and . . ."

Brent stared at the other boy. "He *hooked* me? With his stick?"

"Yeah," Darryl said. "He caught your ankle with it. He's over in the penalty box now. We got a power play out of it anyway."

"Did it look like he tripped me up on purpose? Could you tell?" asked Brent.

Darryl hesitated. He looked at the ice and back at Brent, then finally said, "I don't know. I mean, the guy . . . he's clumsy, you know? So maybe he just lost his balance. I couldn't say. I don't think he was out to hurt you. He just wanted to stop you."

Brent thought about it and realized that Darryl was right. Whatever Vic had wanted to do, the dude hadn't deliberately set out to hurt him. Still, no matter what Vic had *wanted* to do, Brent might well have been hurt when he crashed into the boards.

A couple of minutes later, Coach Maxwell called "Time-out!" and went over to check on Brent. "You ready to come back in?" he asked.

Brent stood up. His upper arm felt a little sore, but otherwise he was fine. "Definitely," he said.

"Right," said the coach, "you're in for Arno after the time-out."

After the time-out, Brent's squad took the puck and Cam brought it across the blue line into their offensive zone. He held it for a moment, looking for an open man. Barry skated out to confront him, but before he got close, Cam sent the puck rocketing behind the goal.

Brent sped after it. But Max left the goalmouth to take the puck away. He tapped it to Burt, who was in as a defenseman. Burt started the puck the other way, taking it toward center ice. Before an offensive play could get along, the whistle sounded. Barry was ruled offside, having crossed the red line before Burt had gotten there with the puck. The squads faced off at the closest circle.

The play moved back and forth without either side being able to score. Chip made one beautiful save on a shot by Ted, sliding across the crease and just getting the end of his stick on the puck before it got into the net.

"One more minute!" called Coach Maxwell as Brent took the puck after Chip had knocked it away from the crease. He gave it to Cam and headed down the ice. Cam passed to Darryl, who had come in a moment earlier. Darryl avoided Vic's poke check and crossed the blue line to center ice, with Brent on his left and Cam on his right. Cam veered behind Darryl, who dropped the puck onto Cam's stick. Cam flicked it to Brent who got across the red line, while Barry tried to force Brent off the puck. Brent fired to Gavin, who moved into the offensive zone and slapped a long shot at the goalmouth.

Max blocked it with his stick, and the puck caromed off to the left of the crease. Cam was the first one to get to the puck. He sent a pass back to Gavin, ten feet in front of the net. Gavin slipped a shot that tumbled into the goal, just over Max's outstretched leg, for the first and only goal of the scrimmage. Gavin's squad-mates gave him a series of high-five and pats on the back.

A few seconds after the face-off that followed, Coach Maxwell blew his whistle and called "Time!" The scrimmage was over.

"Everybody, group up over here," called the coach. When the team was gathered around him, he said, "That was excellent! I saw a lot of good, hard work out there. Good passing, hard checks, and teamwork. Play like that against the Cyclones, and you'll give them a real fight. You should all feel good about what you did today.

"Take a quick break, and we'll use the rest of the time to work on some special plays."

Cam tapped Brent on the shoulder. "You all right?"

"Yeah, it wasn't serious. I feel a little sore, that's all. But I wasn't really hurt."

Ted, who had overheard what Brent said, sarcastically muttered, "Yeah, I guess Vic'll have to try harder next time."

Cam spun around to face the other boy. "Hey! What are you trying to say?"

Ted didn't back off. "Brent could've broken an arm! And you know it!"

"Yeah, well, he didn't! Anyway, what happened was an accident!" snapped Cam.

"An accident, huh?" said Ted. "Is that so? Brent, did Vic come over to ask how you were? Did he say he was sorry?"

Brent shook his head. "No."

"I didn't think he did," Ted said, his eyes fixed on Cam. "You know what? I'm not sure it *was* an accident! That's the kind of dirty play his father wants us all to do! Vic keeps having these 'accidents,' have you noticed? I don't like it!"

"Guys, cool it," Brent said, feeling caught in the middle. "This isn't right."

Ted turned to Brent. "Well, do *you* think it was an accident? Or did he trip you on purpose?"

Both boys looked at Brent, waiting for his answer. Brent wanted, more than anything else, to sound fair.

"I guess Vic isn't the world's greatest skater, and I really don't believe he was out to hurt me."

Cam nodded, and Ted looked angry.

"*But,*" Brent went on, "I also think that when you try to break the rules, it's easier for people to get hurt.

98

And it doesn't matter if it's accidental or on purpose. And that's one of the things I don't like about the way Coach Seabrook wants us to be 'winners.'"

Now it was Ted's turn to look pleased and Cam's to frown.

"That's not fair!" he said. "Coach Seabrook isn't trying to get anyone hurt, and you know it!"

"I didn't say he was *trying* to —" Brent started.

But Ted interrupted. "He says it's okay to break rules as long as you don't get caught! You think that's all right?"

Other players were watching Ted and Cam, whose voices got louder with each exchange.

"He knows how we can be champs." Cam's face was red, and his fists were clenched. "I'm tired of playing with a bunch of *losers!*"

Ted's eyes got wide. "You think we're a bunch of losers, huh? Then why don't you just quit? Who needs you?"

"I'm not going to quit! But maybe you should, if you don't care about winning!"

"Cut it out!" Coach Maxwell stepped between the two boys. He looked at each of them in turn. Both Cam and Ted suddenly looked embarrassed.

Standing in the midst of the players, Coach Maxwell didn't seem angry as much as sad. He ran a hand through his hair and said very softly, "I don't know . . . maybe I don't know this team anymore."

"I'm sorry, Coach," Ted said, "I was totally out of line."

He offered his hand to Cam, who shook it. Cam said, "I didn't mean to yell."

Coach Maxwell said, "I don't know why some of you guys think I don't want the team to win. I know I never said anything like that. Nobody's happier when you win a game than I am. All I've been saying is that I don't see winning as the only important goal. Especially not for people your age. Sports are supposed to be fun. That's the bottom line, I always thought.

"But maybe times have changed, and I'm out of step. If I am . . . then maybe you'd be better off with a coach who'll give you what you want. I don't know."

"*No!*" Brent's shout startled several players, including himself. "Don't talk about that! We need you. You're the one we want to coach the Badgers!"

Several other boys spoke out in agreement. But some didn't say anything at all, and one of the silent ones was Cam.

100

After a moment, Cam spoke. "I don't think anybody wants you to leave, Coach. But if having another guy around can make us better, what's wrong with that? Why shouldn't we be the best team we can be?"

Coach Maxwell smiled, "I want this team to be the best it can be, too, Cam. I guess the question is, what does 'the best' mean?"

Cam blinked, as if he couldn't believe such a dumb question. "The best is the team that wins the most. That's right, isn't it?"

"Seems so to me," said Coach Seabrook.

"Right!" agreed Vic.

"Does anyone have a different opinion?" asked Coach Maxwell.

"If you're playing as well as you can, then you're the best . . . well, the best you can be anyway," Brent said. "That's what I want for my team."

Several boys started talking at once, some agreeing with Cam and others with Brent.

Coach Maxwell held up a hand to quiet everyone down. "I think we need to have a team meeting to talk about this some more," he said. "I want to set it up for tonight, if possible, after dinner. How does that sound?"

The players looked around at each other. Most of them were willing.

"Can parents come, too?" asked Arno.

"I wish they would," Coach Maxwell replied. "I'll arrange a room at the middle school and let people know where and when." He looked at his watch. "Until then, let's wrap it up with some stretching. Everyone, in the locker room."

The team filed off the rink quietly.

Later on, Cam's mother picked up Brent and her own son. There was little talk between the boys on the drive home. Brent was thinking about what was going to happen to the Badgers and whether he'd still feel like it was his team after that evening. He was pretty sure that the same thoughts were going through Cam's mind as well.

Brent hoped that they'd both feel that they were teammates and friends after the meeting was over.

11

Just before dinner, Coach Maxwell phoned the Mullen house to say that the meeting was set for that evening and that parents and boys were urged to be there if they could.

"I don't get it," Lee said, once the family was at the table. "Coach Maxwell has been running the team for a long time, and there were no complaints. What's going on?"

Brent shrugged. "Guess 'winner' is a magic word. When this new coach talks about being winners, a lot of guys start listening, and it sounds good to them."

"*And* to some of the parents, too," added Mr. Mullen. "When we go to the games, there are always a few fathers and mothers around who aren't happy unless their team wins. They don't buy this idea that doing your best is what matters. I remember this one guy who used to say, 'If you're not a winner, then you're a loser.' He'd say it over and over, even when his son's team lost. And his son would hear it, too. I could never understand that."

"But you think Coach Maxwell is going to still be our coach, right, Dad?" asked Brent.

"Sure he will," Lee said.

"Let's put it this way," said Mr. Mullen. "As long as most of the parents want him, Coach Maxwell will be running the team. And while I think there are some parents who would rather see more emphasis put on winning than Coach Maxwell is willing to do, I'm pretty sure that he'll still be running things tomorrow. But I can't say for sure."

Brent didn't feel very hungry all of a sudden. He couldn't imagine Coach Maxwell leaving, but his father seemed to think that it might happen. "I don't want to play for Coach Seabrook if he's in charge. I'd have to quit. And I wouldn't be the only one either."

"Let's not worry about that unless we have to," said Mr. Mullen.

"Tell Coach Maxwell I'm rooting for him," Lee said. "I think it's really gross that some people might want a different man running the team. They don't know what they're doing if they let that happen."

Brent said, "We won't *let* it happen, right, Dad?"

"We'll do what we can," his father answered. "That much, I can promise you."

When Brent and his father arrived at the big room that Coach Maxwell had reserved at the local middle school there were already a lot of people there. Most of the players had come, and almost all of them had brought at least one parent with them. More than half the chairs in the room were full. In the front of the room was a low platform with a few chairs and a microphone.

Brent saw that Cam and his parents were among those present. So were Coach Seabrook and Vic. The parents were gathered in small groups talking quietly. A few boys were talking and laughing, but several of them, including Arno, Chip, Sandy, and Ted, were quiet and serious.

"Where's Coach Maxwell?" asked Brent, looking around the room. "I don't see him."

"He's going to be here, I'm sure of that," said Mr.

Mullen. He checked his watch. "It's a few minutes early yet."

Arno and Ted caught Brent's eye and waved. Brent nodded toward them but stayed with his dad. He didn't feel like talking.

The door opened, and Coach Maxwell walked in. Coach Seabrook and a few parents came up to him, and he shook hands with them and then walked to the front of the room.

He adjusted the microphone and spoke into it. "Can everyone hear me? If everyone would take seats, we can start."

All the conversations stopped. Once everyone in the room was sitting, the coach went on. "First of all, I want to thank everyone for getting here on very short notice. This meeting is a first for me, as it is for all of you, I'm sure. But some questions have come up that need to be discussed, and this will give anyone who wants their opinion to be heard the chance to speak up."

A voice called out, "Who's in charge here? Are you going to run this meeting?" Brent recognized the speaker as Burt's dad. He had a hunch that Burt's dad was one of the people who liked Coach Seabrook's ideas because he didn't sound very friendly toward Coach Maxwell.

"I hadn't thought about that," said Coach Maxwell. "I'm open to suggestions."

"Well, I don't think you should run it," said Burt's dad. "I mean, the main question here is whether you should still coach this team, so I think someone who's neutral ought to be the one to run the meeting."

"Fine with me," said the coach. After a short discussion, Chip's father, Mr. Sullivan, was picked. Mr. Sullivan went to the microphone.

"Uh, let's start by asking each coach to say what he thinks about the direction the team should take. Then anyone who wants to be heard can speak his mind. Coach Maxwell, why don't you begin?"

Coach Maxwell returned to the mike.

"I don't really have much to say. You know me and what I believe in. When you work with boys who are eleven, twelve, thirteen years old, your basic job is to teach hockey skills and technique, and the strategies of the game. I've never placed much emphasis on winning for its own sake, and I'm not about to start now. If I'm still the coach, I'll keep doing what I've always done. Thank you."

He walked away from the mike. A few people clapped.

Brent had hoped for a more emotional speech, something with fire in it that would have swept away opposition to his staying. But Coach Maxwell hadn't spoken for more than a few seconds and hadn't raised his voice.

"Thanks, Coach Maxwell," said Mr. Sullivan, who'd been as surprised as everyone else by the shortness of the coach's speech. "Coach Seabrook, your turn."

The other coach took the microphone.

"Well, most of you *don't* know me, so I'll need a little more of your time. I played hockey for many years, and I've coached for several years. While I agree that a coach has to be a teacher, I think he needs to do more than that. A coach can take a bunch of kids and make something special of them. He can see to it that the boys who play for him have an experience they'll look back on with pride for the rest of their lives. He can make them *tough,* he can make them *competitors* . . . he can make them *winners!*"

Several audience members began to applaud, but Coach Seabrook cut them off.

"I don't know when 'winning' became an ugly word,

but that's what seems to have happened in many people's minds. If you feel that way about winning, then you do *not* want me as your coach.

"The world is a tough place, and I'm not just talking about sports. To succeed, you have to feel confident. You have to stand up for yourself. You can't let anybody walk over you. Sports prepare you to compete in *life* and be a winner in that game, too. The players I coach may not always be the most well-liked kids on the block, but they will always get *respect*. And *they will win*."

Coach Seabrook nodded and walked away from the mike. Several parents — and several players — clapped loudly.

Brent looked at his father and saw concern on Mr. Mullen's face. Coach Seabrook's words had been well received. If a vote were taken now, Brent thought that the new coach might very well get a majority.

Mr. Sullivan addressed the group. "If anyone wants to speak . . . yes, Mr. Wood?"

Brent recognized the man at the mike as Barry's father. He said, "Uh, I want to say that I really admire and respect Coach Maxwell. He's a good man who's done fine things here, and I'm grateful, as we all are. But sometimes, you have to be ready to make a change, and I believe this is one of those times. I think Coach Seabrook can do a lot for my son and all these boys, and I want to give him the chance to do that. Now, he can do them in cooperation with Coach Maxwell, if Coach Maxwell is willing to share the job. Or if he isn't willing . . . well, then, like I say, it's time for a change. That's all I have to say."

Brent turned to his father, wanting him to speak up for Coach Maxwell. "Dad?"

Mr. Mullen nodded and raised his hand.

Mr. Sullivan signaled for him to take the microphone.

Mr. Mullen said, "Before Brent was a Badger, his older brother, Lee, played for Coach Maxwell. I know some of you have older sons who did the same. Lee's still playing hockey. In fact, he's one of the top high school players in the county, maybe the state. He's got a great shot at a scholarship because of hockey.

"I believe — so does Lee — that he owes his success mostly to Coach Maxwell. There are other boys out there who Coach Maxwell made into fine players on high school and college teams. I can give you names if you like. Were the Badgers champions when Lee was with them? No, they were about average, just like they are now. But boys on those teams came away knowing how to shoot, how to pass, all the basic things that make top hockey players. And good citizens, as well.

"Coach Maxwell *does* produce 'winners,' at least what I think of as winners. We'd be making a big mistake to let him get away. I hope we think long and hard and don't do something we'll regret. Thanks."

There was some applause as Mr. Mullen sat back down.

Several other parents spoke after Brent's dad. A few favored Coach Seabrook, others liked Coach Maxwell, while one or two wanted both to work together. Brent thought that the group was evenly split between making a change and keeping things as they had been.

Once everyone who wanted to speak had been heard, Mr. Sullivan took the mike again. He looked puzzled. "It looks like we're not sure what we should do. I'm not quite sure what happens next."

Mr. Mullen said, "The team plays their next game the day after tomorrow. I don't think it would be right to change coaches without a clear majority in favor of it, and certainly not when the boys have a game coming up. So I think we should leave Coach Maxwell in charge for now."

Barry's father, who liked Coach Seabrook, said, "For now, yes. But that doesn't mean forever. I mean, this isn't settled yet."

Coach Maxwell, who had watched the discussion from the side of the room, stood up. "I'd like to say something, if I may."

"Sure," Mr. Sullivan said.

Coach Maxwell said, "I'm grateful for the kind words some of you said about me. And I have no hard feelings towards those who want to make a change. Maybe it's time for a change, it's hard for me to know. What I *do* know is, I don't want to see more of the problems the team has had for the last few days. I don't think a team can work together when it's run by two coaches whose approaches to the game are as different as mine and Coach Seabrook's. And I don't want to risk causing still more bad feelings and difficulty. I've had fun in this job, but I guess this is where I should turn it over to the new man and a new viewpoint. So, after the game against the Cyclones, this will be Coach Seabrook's team. Thank you."

Coach Maxwell walked out of the room, leaving a stunned silence behind him.

12

Brent wanted to yell "*No!* It's not right," but he realized that he couldn't do that. Still, it was hard for him
to believe what he'd just heard Coach Maxwell say.

Behind him, he heard Coach Seabrook say, "This
isn't what I wanted. I thought we would help each
other, that we could work together. I feel really bad
about this."

"Maybe it's for the best," said one of the fathers.

"I don't think it's right, what Coach Maxwell did,"
said another.

Mr. Mullen said, "He was right that he and Coach
Seabrook can't work together. Their attitudes are too
different, and it confuses the team. We already see the
kind of trouble that causes. He wanted to avoid more
of the same."

Mr. Sullivan said, "Well, now it's going to be Coach

113

Seabrook's team. Personally, I think he'll be an improvement."

"I guess we'll see soon enough," said Mr. Mullen. "Let's go, son."

On the way home, Brent stared out the window, saying nothing.

"I know this is a big disappointment," said his father as they got close to home. "Just hang in there for now and see how it goes. If you decide to leave the Badgers, I'll understand and so will Lee."

"How can this happen?" Brent demanded. "Don't they get it? That other guy is bad news!"

"Some people just love the idea of being number one, I guess," said Mr. Mullen. "Just be glad you got started in hockey under Coach Maxwell. Even if you don't play the whole season with the Badgers, there'll be other teams, maybe in school. Just don't give up on hockey."

Brent shook his head. "I won't. I just feel bad about my friends . . . like Cam. How could he think this guy has the right idea?"

Mr. Mullen pulled into their driveway. He reached over and ruffled his son's hair. "Don't let it get you. You never know. Maybe things will still work out."

Brent found that hard to believe.

The next day was the last practice before the game against the Cyclones . . . and the last practice for Coach Maxwell. As the boys gathered to do their stretches, Coach Maxwell said, "Coach Seabrook will be in charge after the game tomorrow. I'm sure he'll do a great job, and I expect you all to give him the same cooperation and attention you always gave me. Now let's get ready for the Cyclones."

The mood of the practice was quiet. The skate-around and the drills — for shooting, passing, and so on — went pretty much as they usually did. Once again, Coach Maxwell spent time practicing with the centers and wings while Coach Seabrook worked separately with the defensemen and goalies. After a break, the two groups got back together for a scrimmage. Each coach ran a squad. Everyone, coaches and players, was being very careful not to lose his temper.

Gavin, the starting center on Brent's squad, controlled the face-off. He dropped a pass back to Arno, one of his defensemen, who hit a backhand pass to Brent. Brent skated across the red line and left a drop pass for Burt to bring into the offensive zone. Gavin looked like he was open, and Burt sent a pass across the ice toward him, but Cam slammed Gavin into the right-side boards before the puck reached him. Gavin looked around for a penalty call, but the acting officials had had their attention focused elsewhere. To Brent, the penalty by Cam had been obvious and deliberate. Cam took the puck and brought it down the ice along the boards. He shot it down the ice, and an official whistled play to a stop.

"That was icing," he called. "Let's have the puck over here."

Icing can only happen when both teams are at full strength. It is called when a player behind the red line sends the puck all the way past the other team's goal line. There's no penalty time involved, and play resumes with a face-off near where the icing was called.

This time, Ted got the puck on the face-off and passed back to Cam. Cam fired over to Sandy near the red line. Brent moved in on Sandy, who sent the puck back to Cam. Arno attempted to check Cam off the puck, but Vic came in from the side and shoved Arno hard, pushing him away from the play. Arno whirled around angrily.

"What was *that* supposed to be?" he yelled.

116

"Keep playing unless there's a whistle!" called Coach Seabrook from the sidelines.

Arno shook his head, looking disgusted.

Cam passed to Ted. Darryl came in on the fly to replace Vic and took a pass from Ted, sending it quickly over to Barry, his squadmate. Barry fired a slap shot that Chip blocked with his stick, but the puck caromed straight to Cam. Before Chip could get back in position, Cam slid the puck into the net for a goal.

As the rest of Cam's squad came over to slap his back and congratulate him, Arno skated over to Brent. "Did you see what happened? That was a foul! Vic should have gone to the penalty box, for sure! There shouldn't have been a goal."

Brent shrugged. "The linesman didn't see it. That happens sometimes."

"It happens too often lately," grumbled Arno. "I think I'm going to quit this team after tomorrow. I don't like what's going on around here, and it's going to get worse."

"I hear you," Brent answered. "I don't know if I'm going to stay or leave."

A few minutes later, Darryl fell heavily to the ice

when it looked like he might have a breakaway. Brent, who was on the bench at the time, wasn't sure what had happened, but Barry had been right behind Darryl just before he fell. Arno, sitting next to Brent, poked him.

"You think Darryl fell down by accident? I bet that was more of Coach Seabrook's new style."

Brent wasn't sure what had happened. What bothered him was that he couldn't say for certain that Arno was wrong.

After practice, he joined Cam outside to wait for their ride. Brent said, "Arno says he's quitting the team."

"Yeah, that's what I heard," Cam answered. "Chip may leave, too."

This was news to Brent. Chip was not only a nice guy, he was by far their best goalie. That would be a major loss for the Badgers.

Cam said, "What about you? *You're* not going to leave, are you?"

Brent realized that he still didn't know what he'd do. He hated the idea of walking out on the team. It made him feel guilty even to think about it. But he also hated playing the kind of hockey that the new coach wanted. He didn't say anything.

"*Are* you?" Cam repeated. "Come on, man, don't quit! We need you. *I* need you. You're making too much of a big deal about this new coach."

"I don't think so," said Brent. "I don't know what I'm going to do yet, but I don't want to play that way. In fact, even if I stay, I'm not going to play that game. And don't tell me to grow up or say welcome to the real world or anything like that. I don't want to hear it."

"Lighten up, all right?" Cam said, looking unhappy. "I didn't say those things."

Brent kicked a pebble off the sidewalk. "All I'm saying for now is I'll be there tomorrow and give it one hundred percent. After that . . . well, I don't know yet."

He really didn't know, and it was too bad.

13

The next day, Mr. Mullen drove to the rink. Brent sat in the back with his equipment piled next to him. Lee sat up front with their father. He glanced at Brent, who hadn't wanted to talk much.

Lee broke the silence. "How are you feeling? Ready for the game, bro?"

Brent said, "Yeah, I'm ready. For the game, that is. I don't know if I'm ready for whatever I'll be doing *after* the game."

"Don't let that other stuff distract you," Lee warned. "Okay? The game comes first."

"I know that!" Brent snapped. Then he sighed. "Sorry. It's just that I . . ."

He didn't know how to finish the sentence.

"I understand," said his brother. "I don't believe this is really going to happen. If I were in your shoes, I'd be going through the same thing. But at least you can give Coach Maxwell a 'W' as a going-away present."

Brent smiled "That'd be great! The Cyclones are tough this year. Three wins, one tie, and no losses. Maybe if we can beat them, people will want Coach Maxwell to stay."

Lee shook his head. "They'll probably say you won because of what the new coach is doing. Their minds are made up, bro. Don't expect any miracles. But beating these guys would be really excellent."

"I'd love to beat them," Brent said, "if we can do it without cheating."

As the Badgers did their pregame stretching, Brent could hear the noise of a few hundred people who had come to watch the game. Usually before the game, there would be a lot of chatter in the locker room. Today it had been very quiet. When the stretching was done, Coach Maxwell stood up and looked at the team.

"The Cyclones are a better team than last year . . . and they beat us then. But you have the talent to win today, if you go all-out and play hard. Remember what we've worked on, keep your heads in the game, and play as a team. Don't worry about tomorrow or anything but what's happening on the rink. Whatever happens today, you should know that I'm proud of you."

Coach Seabrook was next. He wasn't wearing his usual smile. Instead, he glared. "These guys," he said, "they think they're really tough. They think they're better than you. They figure all they have to do is show up, and you'll fold. Send them a message. Make them respect you. Show the people out there that you're *winners*. You know what you have to do, what we've practiced. Go for it!"

The team filed out onto the rink. Brent wondered if he'd ever wear his blue-and-gold uniform again.

The Cyclones were already on the ice, doing their skatearound, wearing black and red. The Badgers did their own warm-up while the coaches for both teams huddled with the referee and two linesmen. As he skated, Brent saw his family sitting behind the red line, only a few seats away from Cam's parents and little sister.

The referee blew his whistle, and the two starting lineups took the ice. For the Badgers, the starting front line had Ted at center with Brent and Sandy at the wings. The defensemen were Cam and Burt, and

Chip was the goalie. As was customary, the players from both teams touched gloves as they lined up for the opening face-off. Normally for Brent, this was a very exciting moment. Today the usual excitement was mixed with sadness.

The whistle sounded again as a linesman dropped the puck. The Cyclone center beat Ted on the draw and slapped the rubber disk to his left, where a defenseman took it. Brent dropped back to defend, keeping his eye on the puck and on the Cyclone wing nearest to him. He saw the play developing across the ice as the Cyclone center and his left winger moved over the red line, passing the puck between them.

The center took the puck between Ted and Sandy and skated it across the blue line. Then he dropped it back to a defenseman and headed toward the crease.

Cam moved in on him, but the Cyclone defender passed to the right wing. Brent moved closer, looking for a chance to knock the puck away or put a check on the player.

Another whistle blew, stopping play. A linesman skated over to the sidelines to explain the penalty he had apparently called. *That was fast,* Brent thought.

An official's voice came over the public address

system: "Number eight, blue, two minutes for inter-ference."

Barry, who had been struggling with a Cyclone wing in front of the crease, had been called for doing something he shouldn't have. Looking as if he'd been caught taking cookies from a cookie jar, he skated over to the penalty box. Less than a minute into the game, the Cyclones had a power-play opportunity.

Coach Maxwell put Brent, Ted, Cam, and Burt in as his penalty-killing unit. Following the face-off — in the circle to the left of the Badger goal — the Cyclones controlled the puck. They began by passing around the perimeter of their offensive zone, looking for an opening, but the Badgers covered well. A Cyclone wing suddenly darted toward the crease, hoping to catch the Badgers by surprise. A perfect, needle-threading pass got to him, but Brent's lightning-fast poke check knocked the puck away, right to where Cam could take it. Cam sent the puck skimming all the way down to the other end of the rink, forcing the Cyclones to use valuable seconds getting it back. Brent heard his brother yell something, but he couldn't make it out.

With under a minute left in the penalty, the Cyclone

center fired a shot to the upper left corner of the goal. Chip took it on his blocker and lunged after the puck as it skittered on the ice. But before he could capture it, a Cyclone wing came around from behind the net and hooked it in for a goal. The Cyclones led, 1 to nothing.

With the score, both teams were at full strength again. Cam and Burt were replaced by Arno and Darryl, and Gavin came in for Ted. Coach Maxwell signaled Brent and Sandy to stay on for another minute.

Even against Gavin, a fresh center, the Cyclones controlled the face-off. But the Cyclone wing closest to Brent tried to get behind the Badger defense and left Brent unguarded. Arno threw a good body check at the opposing center, jarring the puck loose. Sandy got it and fired a perfect pass to Brent, streaking across the red line. Too late, the Cyclone wing saw his own mistake.

Brent outskated the closest Cyclone defenseman and had nobody between him and the Cyclone goalie — a perfect breakaway opportunity. The goalie moved out to try to cut down Brent's shooting angle.

Brent feinted to his right, drawing the goalie over to the side, and then slammed a shot into the upper left corner of the net for the tying goal. It was only his second goal of the season, and it made the score 1–1.

Brent was mobbed by his teammates as he and Sandy came to the bench to be replaced by Vic and Gil. For the next several minutes, neither team was able to score. The Cyclones managed a shot on goal that Chip saved with a sliding stop. Just as Brent was poised to scramble back onto the ice in a change on the fly for Gil, there was another whistle. This time, it was a penalty on Vic for high-sticking.

Brent saw the linesman skate over to the Badger bench, looking angry. "I could just as easily have made this a major penalty for slashing," he told Coach Maxwell. "Tell your guys to watch themselves. They're getting too rough out here."

Coach Seabrook leaned in and began yelling at the linesman as he skated away. Coach Maxwell pulled the other coach back and said something to him that shut him up fast. Meanwhile, Brent went back out on the ice — as part of the Badger penalty-killing unit.

Forty seconds later, the Cyclone center made a beautiful pass to one of his wings, who had taken up a position next to the corner of the Badger goal. Chip managed to deflect the wing's shot but couldn't hang onto the puck, and the center himself poked it in for a goal. The Cyclones now led 2–1 and had scored both their goals on power plays. The period ended with the Cyclones still ahead by a goal.

In the locker room during the break between periods, Coach Seabrook gave an angry talk. "I'm not seeing the kind of spirit I want out of this team! We're not sending these guys a message! Do you want to win or not? If you do, then do what you have to!"

Coach Maxwell's talk was quieter. "It's still our game to win or lose," he said. "Their front lines have a tendency to get themselves out of position. They're looking for odd-man advantages, and that means we could find chances to get another breakaway. Also, you defensemen, don't neglect your defensive responsibilities. Don't get so far into the offensive zone that you can't get back when you need to. Keep your heads in the game."

Brent couldn't tell if either speech had made much of an impact. He found out two minutes into the second period.

Brent was on the bench at the time. The front line was Ted, Gil, and Neil, with Cam and Vic on defense. The Cyclones had advanced across the blue line into their offensive zone, and their left wing had passed to the center, lurking behind the net. Brent was watching the puck when out of the corner of his eye he saw Cam streaking toward the wing who had just passed. The wing was also watching the puck and didn't see Cam until the husky defenseman slammed into him and knocked him against the boards. The boy in black and red slumped to the ice and didn't move.

Someone in the stands screamed. The ref blew his whistle, and everything stopped. Cam stood over the motionless Cyclone player like a statue. The crowd was suddenly silent. But the Cyclone coach was anything but silent.

"That was flagrant!" he yelled. *"He hit him from behind!"*

Two of the officials were now bent over the boy on the ice while the other linesman grabbed Cam by the arm and led him away. Cam seemed dazed.

The Cyclone coach, realizing that his player might be seriously hurt, came out onto the ice followed by Coach Maxwell. The Cyclone coach was yelling at the officials and at Coach Maxwell, who put his arm around the other coach and said something that quieted the angry man. The boy on the ice had not yet moved. Brent couldn't tell whether he was conscious or not.

A few minutes later, a stretcher was wheeled onto the ice. The boy was gently lifted onto a board and then onto the stretcher and quickly taken out of the rink. Brent saw a man and woman hurry out of the stands to follow the stretcher. The boy's parents, he assumed. Everyone in the arena had stood up and clapped, saluting the injured player.

At the side of the rink, the Cyclone coach whispered to another man, who nodded and also left.

Now the officials called over the coaches of both teams and had a brief conversation. At one point, Brent heard Coach Seabrook say, "But that's not fair! You didn't see what happened!"

The referee stuck a finger under coach Seabrook's nose, and whatever he said silenced the coach immediately. Now the announcer spoke over the public address system.

"Number five of the blue team" — that was Cam — "has been given a game misconduct, and the red team will receive a penalty shot. Because the player who was hit is unable to take the penalty shot, it will be taken by a substitute."

Cam had been kicked out of the game. As for the Cyclone who'd been hit, word spread that he'd been taken to a local hospital. It wasn't clear how badly he was hurt. Coach Maxwell put his arm around Cam, who still appeared to be stunned. The coach walked Cam into the locker room. Cam's father followed them.

A few minutes later, the substitute Cyclone took the penalty shot. Brent held his breath until Chip blocked his shot with a glove, and play resumed.

Neither team played with much energy; it was obvious that what had happened had taken the steam out of everyone. When the Badgers went to the locker room after the second period, Cam and his father were gone. Coach Seabrook tried to make another go-get-'em pep talk, but nobody paid much attention. Arno muttered, "Guess we know what he means by 'sending them a message,' don't we?"

The third period was a disaster for the Badgers. The final score was 4–2 Cyclones.

Coach Maxwell said, "I'm going to the hospital to see how that boy is. "I'll let people know as soon as I have information."

Coach Seabrook said, "I'd like to say that what happened was very unfortunate, but accidents sometimes happen in hockey. I hope you boys weren't too upset, and I'm sure that young man is going to be just fine tomorrow."

Everyone left quickly.

14

In the car, Brent said, "Can we go to Cam's house?"

Mr. Mullen frowned. "I don't know if that's a good idea, son."

Brent replied, "I'd really like to."

"Tell you what," said his father. "I'll stop and see if they're up for a visit. All right?"

"Fine," Brent said.

At the Johanssen house, Mr. Mullen rang the doorbell and went inside. A moment later, he came back to the car.

"Cam wants to see you. I'll drive home with Lee. Call if you need me later. And, son?"

Brent had opened his car door. "Yeah?"

"I'm proud of you. This is a thoughtful thing to do. He needs a friend tonight."

Brent nodded and went to the open door. He found Mr. Johanssen in the hall.

"Hey, Mr. J., how's Cam doing?"

Cam's dad managed a weak smile. "Not great but glad you're here. He's in the den."

Brent found his friend on a couch, staring at the floor. "Hey, dude," Brent said. "Okay to sit down?"

"Sure," Cam said. "You hear anything about how that guy is?"

"Not yet." Brent sat across from Cam. "Oh yeah, not that it matters now, but we lost."

"Uh-huh."

"Coach Maxwell is at the hospital. He'll let everyone know when there's news."

Cam kept his eyes on the floor. He said, "I wanted to go to the hospital to see how he was and apologize, but Dad said it wasn't a good idea. Maybe tomorrow."

"Maybe," Brent said, hoping that the boy would be in shape for visitors by then.

Cam looked at Brent. "I didn't mean to hurt him."

Brent nodded. "I know."

"I was only . . . the coach said to send them a message!

I wanted to . . . make them respect us. But I didn't . . . I wish I hadn't done it!"

Mr. Johanssen looked in. "Can I get you boys anything? Something to eat or drink?"

"No, thanks," Brent said. Cam shook his head. A phone rang, and Mr. Johanssen said "I'll get that" and left the room.

Cam slumped back on the couch. "You must think I'm a total jerk. *I* think I am."

"I don't, and you're not," Brent said. "What happened tonight was really terrible. But anyone might have done what you did."

Cam said, "Oh, yeah? *You* wouldn't have done it."

"Well . . . probably not," admitted Brent. "But I have an older brother who taught me what to do and not to do. A lot of guys on the team were ready to 'send a message' tonight. Don't be too hard on yourself."

"If that guy is, like, really hurt . . . I don't know what I'll do."

Mr. Johanssen came in and sat by his son. "That was Coach Maxwell on the phone."

Both boys stared at the man.

"He says that the boy will be fine. He's awake, and there's no serious damage. They're keeping him for observation, so if you want to see him tomorrow, son, that would be all right."

Cam took a deep breath and said, "Oh, man. Am I happy to hear *that*."

Cam's father went on. "I also asked Coach Maxwell if there was a chance that he might reconsider and stay with the team. I think he'd be willing."

"You mean he'd work with Coach Seabrook?" Brent asked.

"I mean *instead* of Coach Seabrook," Mr. Johanssen replied, looking grim. "I'm setting up another parents' meeting, and I think the result will be very different. In fact, I'll guarantee it. You boys aren't the only ones who learned from what happened tonight. Grown-ups make mistakes, too. Bigger ones because we ought to know better. But we can learn from them, and I'm pretty sure most of us did."

A few nights later, in the same meeting room, there was a similar gathering of parents and players. There were several more people than the previous time.

Neither Coach Maxwell nor Coach Seabrook was there when Brent and Cam and their fathers arrived.

Mr. Johanssen went to the front of the room. "If I can have everyone's attention —"

"Where's Coach Maxwell?" someone called out.

"I expect him any moment," replied Cam's father. "I know he's willing to continue as the Badgers coach, and I also assume that we want him back. Does anyone want to discuss this?"

"What about Coach Seabrook?" called out another father. "Is he coming back?"

"I can only speak for myself," said Cam's father. "I don't accuse Coach Seabrook of wanting anyone to get hurt, but I saw all I wanted to of what he calls being 'winners' the other night. I wouldn't want Cam playing if he was going to continue as a coach. My guess is, he knows enough not to even try."

Barry's father, who had been in favor of Coach Seabrook at the first meeting, got up to speak. "I made a mistake the other night, and now I'm willing to admit it. After what happened, I realize that Coach Maxwell is the kind of man I want running my boy's team."

"Anyone opposed to bringing Coach Maxwell back?" asked Mr. Johanssen.

Nobody said a word.

"Well, that's that," he said. "Now as soon as —"

The door opened, and Coach Maxwell walked in. With him came two other people: a young man Brent didn't recognize and Vic Seabrook. Vic looked very nervous.

Mr. Johanssen came forward and shook Coach Maxwell's hand. "We already took a vote, Coach. We want you back, if you're still willing to return."

"I'd be happy to," said the coach. "I'd like to say a few words, if I may."

"There's the mike," replied Mr. Johanssen.

"Thank you," said Coach Maxwell. "First of all, I'd like to say that I know that everyone regrets what happened at the game the other night, and we're all thankful that nobody suffered a serious injury. I think it's important to remember what happened but not to dwell on it. Let's move on from there and not get involved with pointing fingers or assigning blame."

The coach waved the young man who'd come in with him to his side. "This is Evan Halliwell, who played on my first Badger team several years ago. Evan went on to play college and semi-pro hockey, and now he teaches physical education not far from here. He's kindly agreed to work as my assistant coach. I know he'll be helpful and that he'll teach the boys a lot.

"Also, I asked Vic here if he wanted to continue with the team. He wasn't sure he'd be welcome after what happened, but I told him that I was sure that everyone realized that he wasn't to blame in any way. I expect him to be treated like everyone else on the team."

Vic looked up at Coach Maxwell and smiled.

"Does anyone have any questions or anything they want to say?" asked Coach Maxwell.

Mr. Johanssen cleared his throat. "Uh, only that everyone is really happy to have you back, Coach. And I'm sure we all want to welcome Evan and Vic as well."

The coach nodded and smiled.

"That's that, then. Okay, all I have to say is that our next practice is the day after tomorrow, and we have a lot to do, so all you boys had better get your rest and be ready to go to work."

Brent thought that it was the greatest thing he'd ever heard.

Matt Christopher®

Muhammad Ali

Lance Armstrong

Kobe Bryant

Jennifer Capriati

Dale Earnhardt Sr.

Jeff Gordon

Ken Griffey Jr.

Mia Hamm

Tony Hawk

Ichiro

LeBron James*

Derek Jeter

Randy Johnson

Michael Jordan

Peyton and Eli Manning*

Yao Ming

Shaquille O'Neal

Jackie Robinson

Alex Rodriguez

Babe Ruth

Curt Schilling

Sammy Sosa

Tiger Woods

THE #1
SPORTS SERIES
FOR KIDS

Read them all!

*Previously published as Crackerjack Halfback

All available in paperback from Little, Brown and Company

**Previously published as Pressure Play
*Coming in Fall 2008